DOWN, OUT AND DEAD

DOWN, OUT AND DEAD

A collection from Down & Out Books' Authors

EDITED BY
ERIC CAMPBELL

Down & Out Books
3959 Van Dyke Rd, Ste. 265
Lutz, FL 33558
www.DownAndOutBooks.com

Cover design by J.T. Lindroos

ISBN: 1937-4958-1-7

ISBN-13: 978-1-937495-81-7

For Christy, Anthony & Trevor

CONTENTS

Introduction
Eric Campbell

Damn, it's hard to believe that Down & Out Books has published fifty-nine books thus far. And I'm far from done.

For those who don't know, I started D&OB over three years ago after investing and working with Ben LeRoy and Alison Dasho at Tyrus Books. After we sold Tyrus, a burning need to contribute in some small way to the crime fiction genre I so enjoy burned strongly. I blame Jon and Ruth Jordan for fanning the flame by allowing me to publish the ebook edition of Crimespree Magazine.

People often ask how I'm able to juggle a demanding day job, a family and still find time to chase my passion. I tell you this: if it weren't for the support and strength of my family—thank you Christy, Anthony and Trevor—I would not have jumped into D&OB with both feet. They are the best!

This collection came about while speaking with a few of the folks I have published. They *encouraged* me to put together this collection as a way to say thanks to the reading community for three wonderful years.

In closing, thank you, Constant Reader. Thanks to Sandi Loper for her assistance. Thanks to J.T. Lindroos for providing a great supply of wonderful covers. And thank you to the Authors who placed their faith in D&OB and me.

I am humbled and forever grateful.

Tourettes
Les Edgerton

Claude's was the best place we could go, if we were gonna go out in public, Tommy explained, on the way over. "No honkies go in there hardly ever. Anybody recognizes us from the TV ain't gonna give us up. They got that black code. Plus, we all look alike to the brothers."

I wasn't too sure about any black code, but what the hell.

When we went in, sure enough—there's about twenty-five black brothers and the noise level went down appreciably the second we walked in. Tommy fetched us a couple of brewskies from the bartender while I used the coin phone in the back to call Cat and tell her where we were and invite her to join us, which she said she might, and we went on back to a booth. After a couple of minutes and some looks from the brothers I wasn't crazy about, things seemed to go back to normal. Somebody played the juke box and B.B. King began to sing.

"Tommy," I said. "I guess I'm with you on this deal—way I see it, I got no choice. But, I have to wonder if you've covered all the bases here. If you've told me everything, for instance."

"What else would there be?" he said. "Have I ever held anything out on you in our partnership, Pete?"

"Well," I said. "I wasn't aware we had a partnership, but yeah, you have held stuff out on me before." I leaned forward until my face was a foot from his. "Why the fuck didn't you tell me ol' Fred ran a Mafia laundering operation?"

"You think I knew that? I look stupid?"

I leaned back, turned my head like I was talking to the imaginary person sitting to my right. "This is too easy," I said. "I'll leave this one for an amateur."

Tommy looked contrite. "Look," he said. "I know I fucked up. But now I got the solution. Deneuvé."

I was having second thoughts about that. No, make that third and fourth thoughts.

"Oh, that's swell, Tommy. Now my mind is at ease. For a minute there, I thought I was a dead man."

He flashed me a smile. "Only one thing is gonna get us out of this alive. My plan."

"Yeah," I said. "Or the Second Coming."

We had us a second beer each—Tommy had to go up to the bar as it looked like the waitress was on break—and he laid out some of the other details. He was just finishing up with all that and the door opened and in sashayed Cat, hips swinging.

That got a reaction from the crowd. There was a hitch in the noise level and I could see the brothers stare and the sisters dig elbows into their dates. Looked like we were really on the radar now.

"Hey, Cat," Tommy said.

"Hey, Tommy. Hey, Pete." She slid in beside Tommy. So that's the way it was going to be.

"What's your pleasure, Miss?" It was the bartender. Come to wait on us.

She shined him all of her teeth. "You wouldn't have Parfait Amore, would you, sugar?" she said. The only thing left off of her Scarlett O'Hara impression was batting her eyelashes. Pulling down her top a couple extra inches to show off her twins probably made up for that.

"Ah," the barkeep said. "The Drink of Love. I'm sorry, no."

"That's all right," Cat said. "I'll have Black and White, neat, water back."

"From my bottle to your glass," said the bartender and whirled around like a matador and quickstepped back to behind the bar and began pouring.

I looked down at mine and Pete's beers, both empty.

The bartender returned with Cat's two glasses.

Tommy looked up at him and tried to match Cat's smile. "Uh," he said. "You suppose my friend and I could get a refill?"

The best way I could describe how the bartender looked at him was "frosty." "I'm a bartender, not a waiter, Slick," he said, and stalked away.

Tommy shot me a "fuck me" look and shook it off. "Look," he said to me. "I've got some more stuff to do before tonight"—here he narrowed his eyes and furrowed his brow at me like I was supposed to pay special attention to what he was saying—"and I'll see you back at 'the place' at six, Pete. Six. O'clock. Got it?"

He stood there waiting until I repeated his instructions.

"Yeah, Tommy. Six o'clock. I'll set my alarm."

He nodded, gave Cat a little salute, and walked to the door and out.

Cat smiled. "When Tommy told me about you, he said you used to play baseball, Pete. Did you ever meet Mickey Mantle or Babe Ruth?"

I guess this was her version of chit-chat and socializing.

I leaned forward, put my head in my hands. "Mantle and Ruth? Oh, yeah. We was all teammates. Back when baseball was fun." With Tommy gone, I was starting to have buyer's remorse about this kidnap plan. "Right now," I went on, more to me than to her, "I'm in a rundown between third and home. You got any idea what Tommy's brilliant scheme is that we're supposed to do?"

She gave me a coy little smile and stirred her drink. "I think so," she said. "He's grabbed some rich dude. Tommy's a smart guy. We're all gonna be rich."

We? Tommy had neglected to fill me in on the part where Cat was involved in his plan. I was just about to quiz her on that, in a particularly witty and cutting way, when the front door of the bar opened, letting in a shaft of brilliant New Orleans' afternoon sun.

And Sam Capelli.

At first, I didn't realize it was him, not paying strict attention like I shoulda been. He was halfway back before it dawned on me who it was. I flopped down below the table, like I had dropped my change, going down quicker'n vanilla ice cream off a sugar cone in August.

"What?" said Cat, and I yanked on her Capris, and whispered, "It's Sam. Capelli. You know him, you said. He sees me, the only thing left to do is make the funeral arrangements. What the hell's he doin' here? They don't serve no pasta here. God! Let me know what he does."

What he does is plunk his large ass in the booth right next to ours. Cat don't hafta tell me. When he plopped his butt on the seat, he did it with such force the edge of my seat smacked me on the head so hard I saw stars. I almost yelped, but kept it in by biting my lip in half. I sat there with blood running down my chin and tears in my eyes from the pain.

Now I was in it but good. I'm sitting on the floor under the table in a booth in a black bar with a hooker the only thing between me and Doctor Death. There was other places I would rather be at, just then. I couldn't stay down there for the rest of my life; somebody was sure to take note of the honky on the floor, that is, if Cat didn't blow the whistle first, to save her own ass.

Just then, she leaned over with an evil leer and whisper, "I shouldn't do this, asswipe, but I feel sorry for you. I'll get you out of here."

"How?" I whispered back. If she had an idea could spring me out of this jam, I'd go pick out the ring tomorrow, order the tux.

"I'll create a diversion. When I do, you slip out the back, get my car and park up the block. I'll be along presently." She reached into her purse and took something out and handed it to me. Car keys. "It's the red Buick convertible."

What was she going to do? I wondered. Take her clothes off? I couldn't think of much else she could do to not only get Sam but the other twenty-five black guys not to notice me go out the back.

What she did do, I wouldn't have guessed in a thousand years.

She didn't take her clothes off.

She stood up and she threw a fit.

I mean, *she threw a fit.*

She starts yelling and screeching and wandering around the bar, and screaming out all kinds of derogatory things about our black brethren. Like, she said the N word. A bunch of times. "Cocksucker!" she yelled. "Mufucker! N-nigger! F-Fuck. Mutha, mutha, mutha... fuck! Nigger! Whoop!"

You coulda drove a fork lift into my mouth, it was that far open.

"Pussy, pussy, pussy! Whoop! Whoop, whoop, whoop! N-nigger! Shit! Fuck!"

She was in high gear now. All I could see from the floor was black guys moving toward her from all corners.

She kind of staggers up toward the front door, giving out with the insults, and it ain't two seconds before she's drawn a major crowd around her. From under the booth I see a dozen or more black dudes, most of whom have things flashing in their hands, like razors and knives and other sharp and dangerous objects. It appears as if we're about to have a honky woman massacre. The booth shoots back again as Sam gets up and catches me up alongside the head again, and I chomp half my tongue off this time, but keep the sound effects down, just barely. It probably don't matter; there is so much noise and babble up at the front of the bar by now nobody woulda heard me anyway, everybody present with the same fierce desire to be the first to smack Cat, separate her from her gizzard.

Then, I caught on, almost too late. This was the diversion she was talking about, giving me a chance to slip away out the back door. I couldn't figure out how she planned to walk away from this, being as how she was using every racial epithet any cracker had ever thought up. I hoped she knew what she was doing, but it sure looked like a suicide mission from where I was. Might as well one of us get out alive, I thought, and crawled out fast. Nobody paid me any attention, they was all up front, trying t'get at Cat and rip her apart, I figured, and I silently wished her luck and made for the back door. As I was going out, I heard her voice above the murmur of the men, and she was screeching, "Tourette's; I got Tourette's. It's a disease." I shoulda split, soon as I was clear of that door, but I hung around a minute and listened.

"Man, I hearda that," a man's voice said. "It was on TV," said another. "Oprah, I think." "Yeah, poor bitch can't help herself," said still another, and another voice, I could swear it was Sam, said, "My brother-in-law has that, always yelling cusswords and stuff when he gets an attack," and then I was gone, whipping out through the back parking lot, knocking over a couple of garbage cans I didn't stay around to pick up. I ran the whole way till I got to the car, grabbed the keys out of my pocket, jumped in, and started it up.

I did like she said, pulled past the bar and parked about half a block up.

The door of Claude's burst open and a wave of black humanity poured out. Black except for the white hooker and Sam The Bam, who were way in the back taking up the rear of the mob.

Then, the damnedest thing happened. Three or four black dudes were around Cat, and it looked like they were slapping her on the back and hugging her. No, they must be stabbing her. No; by golly, they were patting her on the back and hugging her! I put the car in reverse and rolled toward her. When I got close, I leaned over and opened her door and pushed it out, trying to keep the car in the middle of the street, and just as I came abreast of her, I honked the horn and yelled, "Hit it, Cat! Jump in!"

She waved at me and took a bottle of beer a smiling brother handed her and just sauntered over to me. She climbed in the car and just as she gets in, I hear a voice I don't wanna never hear again in my life, yelling. It was Sam. He was trying to knock guys down and they were turning when he elbowed them but then got polite and got out of his way when they saw his gun.

"Better kick it, slick," Cat said.

I was half a beat ahead of her, the car already leaving rubber and fishtailing as I floored it.

Bam! Bam! Bam!

I look in the rearview mirror and see Sam standing in the street, a two-handed grip on his piece just like Dirty Harry.

A slug hit the rear window and it shattered just before I turned the corner on two wheels. I flew through a stop sign and we almost got broadsided by a huge, oncoming garbage truck, but I drove around him and got clear.

"How... how the hell..." I couldn't get the words together.

Cat was laughing so hard she started to choke. She wiped tears from her eyes. "I always wanted to try that!" she said.

"Try what?" I said. "What in holy hell was all that back there?"

I went up Terpsichore, went under the Ponchartrain Express and turned left on Thalia, taking that on up to Magazine. I turned left onto the Street of Dreams.

I looked over at Cat, trying to spot bruises, contusions, slash marks, but she's clean as a newborn, not a scratch on her.

"What happened, Cat?" I said, and she starts laughing so hard I thought she'd bust her bra.

"I saw Digger O'Henry do that one time in a bar over on Camp Street," she said. "He bet a bunch of other hillbillies he could go into this black bar and call 'em all niggers and they'd end up buying him a drink. He done just what I did; went in this joint and starts yelling out all kinda names that black folks don't normally go for, and then goes into this 'Tourette's' thing. I'll be damned if don't everybody believe him and they end up buying him drinks and wanting to know where they can send money for the Tourette's fund."

"I'll be damned," I said. "They went for that lame shit?"

"Well... not really," she said. "I think they was just playing along with a good-looking woman. I figure they just played along 'cause I showed some balls."

"Fuck me," I said. "Just, fuck me. I am a dead man no matter what I do."

"You're the 'glass is half-empty' type, aren't you?" she said, her smile fading. "Your song is already getting old. Turn left here."

Excerpt from Les' newest novel, THE GENUINE, IMITATION, PLASTIC KIDNAPPING.

Pink Moon
Trey R. Barker

Theirs is the love I've always wanted.

Never found it but, hey, hope springs eternal.

Sweet and romantic and tough and realistic and wildly ambitious. Sometimes, late at night, off-duty and alone in my empty house, what those two have leaves me breathless. Believe that? A big tough cop like me? Damned dogs looking up at me and wondering what the fuck was banging around in my head.

Between them it burns with the blinding white of magnesium on fire. They are as deeply connected as you can possibly imagine. Soul to soul with nothing between them except the rest of time.

Well... except that one other thing.

Her goddamned husband.

"He ain't coming," I say.

"Your mama bash you with a frying pan? That why you're so dumb?" Stone-faced, Craig held up a finger. "Beats on her when dinner is late." A second finger. "Humiliates her with friends, commenting on her body and how good she is in bed." A third finger. "Shoves his hands down her pants to make sure she doesn't smell like another man." Craig's jaw grinds. "Control freak like that?" Craig's laugh is half-croak, half-fear. "He'll be here."

Craig's fiery nerves scare me. Three nights ago he talked about a talking-to. Two nights ago it was a simple tune-up like what Hubby has peppered her with. Last night it was hard bop on Hubby's head. I may be dumb old beat cop, but I can see the escalation.

And now, as the minutes slip past, my gut tightens.

Craig doesn't put his hand on his gun or crack his knuckles, but the growing tension chokes me. Yanks out his cell, speed dials, says, "Not single. Never gonna be single," hangs up.

To me, says, "Billy-A said Hubby was meth-freak-twitchy when he told Hubby she had a lover."

Billy-A... bowling alley clerk. Knew which lanes we loved, knew which lanes we hated. Always gassed us with at least first game. Bowled a two-ninety and knew everyone downtown, bankers to burglars. We'd snatched up our share of bad boys based on Billy-A knowing or hearing.

Craig clenches hands to fists, eyes hard on her loft. It's above an abandoned warehouse just down the street from where we stand. He rented the space and they fixed it up together. It's where they go. To be with each other when they can, to sniff the air of each other when they can't.

A light is on. Like a cheap movie, a shadow moves behind flimsy sheer curtains.

Confusion bangs my head. She's not supposed to be here.

"Shit," I say.

Something squeezes my heart.

And balls.

"It's not on the rocks." Craig into his phone again. "Not a disaster. It's perfect. Edenic, even. Strong as steel." A pause. "Yeah? Well... that was a lie."

Snaps it shut, carries it tight in a fist.

Three years partners. Since Jello—my former partner— chased a two-bit purse snatcher down a blind alley, bought a .45 through the right eye. Craig came next and we been glued since.

We're night shift. Big, faceless metropolis. Get all the dregs the streetscape can toss at us. Drunks and junkies, suicides hanged, suicides shotgunned. Pimps and pederasts and punks. Just so much unwashed bullshit rolling down the gutter before emptying into the bay.

First night out, three years ago, I splashed in that gutter.

"Shit gets on my boots." Not so much as ten words between us from beginning of shift. Trying to shake Craig up, get him to say something.

Stared at me. Finally, "Stay outta the gutter, then, you stupid fuck."

Eyeballed him. Older guy. Got into copping late in life but had been up and down the pipe five or six times already.

"What?" Stared at me. "Step in shit then surprised you stink?"

Laughed so hard I squeezed a couple'a drops out. Friends ever since.

Already four years gone with her when I got him. So tonight, as the moon blasts a brilliant white between the buildings, he's got seven years invested with her. Seven years to a married woman... a woman who, by definition, will never have enough time for him, will never be able to give him what they both want.

But who never stops trying.

She works downtown, accounts payable for a freight firm. Tells Hubby she brown-bags it and instead goes to their loft. Craig had lived in an apartment in the 'burbs. Rented the loft when he was trying to push her to move out, to get a quick D from Hubby and invade Craig's life permanently. Got this loft because it was near where she worked.

He cooks every damn day. Works midnight shift, off at six in the blessed a.m., and is up and cooking for her by eleven. Lunch M - F for four years. And sometimes? When he gets off in the morning, he'll make a surprise visit. No quickies, nothing like that—at least as far as he tells me—but fifteen or twenty minutes together just talking. Or holding hands and watching the early morning, the moon still hanging while the sun creeps up.

Pink moon, colored by a rising sun.

Told me once they fell in love under a pink moon. She'd been a victim of an early morning mugging. She called the cops from her job. Craig and his FTO had handled the call; took the report, handed the case off to the overnight detectives. But he had been smitten. Going back to her, asking how he could help, asking if she remembered anything else, asking anything he could think of while trying to stay inside the professional lines and yet let her know he wanted to go far, far outside those lines. Four or five weeks later, Craig and his FTO stumble across a junkie passed out in the middle of the damned road. They rouse him and lo and behold! Said junkie is wearing her rings, watch, and sleeping on her umbrella.

Craig makes the bust, photog's the evidence, takes everything back to her, and plays the hero's role.

She kissed his cheek and, awkwardly I'm sure, they stood around and talked for a while. On the loading dock of her job, nobody around, the moon hanging full and pink above them. Her face purple with the bruises Hubby had put down the night before. Told me he'd realized at that moment it wasn't love yet but it was marching down that road.

"We found each other that morning," he'd told me. "I'm not even really sure we knew we were missing anything. And then, boom, everything was fine."

Tonight? Maybe not so fine.

Tonight, maybe they were too deep into each other's heads and hearts.

Cell rings. Snaps it open. "Yeah? No, I'm sorry, baby. I wish you were. There are lots."

Craig is my partner and she is his. If he—we—need to step in the shit to save her from a hubby who refuses to divorce her, who's tied up everything of hers in his own name, who isolates her... I'm good with that. Hubby is an abuser, a malcontent, never happy, wants more but wants it handed to him. Spends money like it's fucking going outta style. Talks about getting his own promotions but forced her to quit a previous job when she started doing well and got a promotion or two.

Yeah, I'm good with putting a foot in the stink.

But I'm afraid Craig is going to jump headfirst into the stink.

What if Craig is lying to me? Or she's lying to him? What if home life is hunky dory and she just wants different sheets beneath her ass? Could be Hubby was a perfectly righteous guy who simply had a wife who wants out.

Except I'd seen the bruises...

... the bloody bandages.

I'd driven Craig to the hospital and both back to their loft.

So... Hubby deserves a tune up.

"Tired of waiting," he says.

I swallow. Waiting is what cops do. Most of the time, ninety-eight percent, we're waiting on something to happen. The rest of the time it does happen and we're swirling around in a mess. "A little tune up," I say. "Word to the wise. 'Asshole, quite beating on her.' That'll get it."

Craig ignores me, stares at the loft, at the dark street. Licks his lips. "Been waiting a while."

Tonight, I wanna ask. Or generally?

Cell rings again, a tiny smirk on Craig's face. Answers, says, "Everywhere, Lola. City's got two million people." Pauses. "Yes, ma'am." Pauses. "No, ma'am... I'm sorry."

Three years partners and I know what he's gonna say before he thinks the words, what he's gonna do before he thinks the actions. Except tonight... except in this situation. I have no idea what his plan is.

"That'll get it," I say. "Maybe break a finger."

Closes phone and stares at her loft. "Maybe." Flat affect.

Two hours ago Craig passed word, Billy-A as conduit, to Hubby. Hubby was knocking back pins and brews.

"... gots a lover."

"... gots a loft."

"... gots lunches and walks early in the morning."

"... gots lots'a sex. Wheeeww, baby, lots'a sex."

Billy-A's tinny voice over his shitty track phone said Hubby lost his mind. Smashed his beer bottle against the floor, hurled a bowling ball down the gutter, howled until his voice was ragged.

Craig keys our squad car mic. "Dispatch... 312 out on foot patrol."

"312... 10-4."

Slip outta the cruiser, head toward the warehouse, toward their loft. Near midnight, clouds hanging heavy over everything. Rumble of heavy trucks in and out of downtown, drive/park, deliver to warehouses, smaller trucks outta those warehouses and all over town with product for the buying masses.

We're just two cops, foot beat, rattling doors, checking windows, doing our duty.

The set up? She's in the loft, a night with the unnamed lover. Hubby can nail both in whatever manner he chooses. Truth? She's miles from here, stashed in a hotel under a fake name, waiting to see what's what.

My throat as dry as the fucking Sahara Desert. My hands shaking like an old man staring at a young, beautiful girl.

Because there is someone in her loft.

'Cause right now, Craig's got me plenty scared.

Not rattling doors. Not checking windows. Not nodding to truck drivers, or saying shit to warehouse managers lost in a blue fog of cigarette break smoke. Eyes hard ahead, Hubby's name quiet on his lips, phone against his ear. "Yes. Every word... a lie." Pauses. "I don't know. Five? Eight, maybe? Maybe more."

Hands clenched. Jaw clenched.

"Craig, listen to me. Don't be stupid here. Wanna knock him around? I got no problem with that." Sweat drowning me.

Craig swallows. Hesitates. "Listen, Lola. Something else, too." Bites his lip, walk slows. "I gotta tell you and I'm sorry, but... He's got the worm." Squeezes eyes shut, then snaps them open. "Years... spraying it all over town. I'm sorry. Huh? Fuck, yeah, he knew."

Doesn't look sorry. Looks tight. Looks violent. Looks ready to war.

"Damnit, Craig," I say. "If you wanna break his finger or crack a rib or two the fucker deserves that. But let's don't get too far off the reservation."

Snaps the phone closed and do I hear someone crying—wailing—on the other end just before the hang up? Keeps walking, never turns back to me. "Don't trust me?"

"The fuck is Lola?" I ask. "What's going on?"

Stops, whirls on me. "Moved out." Craig's head snaps up,

a country-bumpkin tourist awed by the big city's tall buildings. His eyes seek out the loft, hard to see from this angle. "From the loft." Eyes come hard to me. "Months ago."

She's gone and moved on as far as the lease is concerned. But the new tenant had been conjured from downtown's polluted air, from the hopes and dreams of my partner and his partner. First and last months' deposits, references ready-made, deal consummated through the mail, key sent and tenant moved in... never seen but there in every way except reality.

"Lola?"

Grins, shakes his head, whispers, "Everybody's got secrets."

A car stops in front of the warehouse, man climbs out, drunk and staggering, yelling and mumbling.

"Even him." Craig says, staring at the man.

Hubby. Headed upstairs. Headed up to take care of his problem.

"And you know them."

Billy-A, Craig tells me.

We wait a few minutes, watching Hubby into the warehouse, then just chilling. Long enough for him to get to the loft, I realize. Then we go in. We stop at the door to the freight elevator. Empties onto a back alley. The alley is stained, dirty, smells like...?

Like the gutter from that night three years ago.

Shake my head. "What the fuck is going on, Craig. What are you doing?"

Raises his hands, palms out, an image of innocent and innocence.

Into the elevator we go. Craig stares at the door, sweat dripping his face, reflecting black in the dim light. Reminds me of blood.

Every moment up, every floor we pass, my guts both tighten and threaten to erupt. This is not what I'd signed on for, not what I'd thought the night would bring. Easiest thing in the world to back down, to back out, flee down the shit-smelling alley like the coward I truly am.

But hardest thing in the world, too.

Craig is my partner, my second half. He completes me in a way no other partner ever has. He is the partner every cop dreams of yet almost none ever get. Unquestioning in front of anyone else, more than willing to bust my nose when we're alone. Always backs my play, always gives me a second or third play to choose from.

Stood by me when the excessive force complaint came along, when the official misconduct complaint came along, when my mother's death came along... a death helped along by a son who could no longer stand to see her in pain or forgetting herself and her soul.

I'll be by his side. I'll give him what he gave me.

Regardless.

Wipe my face, sweat covering my like a sloughing second skin. Rolling down my back, between my checks and down my legs.

And the elevator stops.

When the sound dies, the clank and clang of an industrial lift, there is nothing.

Except... maybe something.

The door opens and we hear it, full of fury.

"The fuck do you think you are? You told me it was over. You told me she was a bitch who hated you. You told me—" A slap and someone falling to the floor. "You told me you were leaving and coming home to me."

"I *am*. What are you saying? Of course, I am coming home to you."

"When? You keep saying that but you never say when. I need to know *when*."

Look at Craig. He glances at his watch, swallows visibly, leans his head to the left to check the shoulder mic on his radio. Lots of chatter, none for us.

"You lying piece of shit. Have you lied about everything?"

"Liar? You calling me a liar?" The voice, deepening now, now an in control male. "Ain't no bitch anywhere calls me a liar."

"Fucking liar," the woman says. Screams, her voice piercing the air all the way down the hallway.

I take a step. Craig holds me back. "Nothing to see here."

"A domestic."

"Just sounds like an argument to me."

"Who the hell is that? Why are they in you guys' loft?"

Craig shakes his head. "Not our loft. Moved out months ago. Hubby must have found out about us, come looking for us."

"I'll beat your ass, bitch. I'll beat your ass back into the kitchen. Or back into the bedroom. You'll apologize."

"*Fuck you!*" absolute rage now. High and exploding. "You got the worm? You fucking gave me AIDS? And how many girlfriends you got? All over fucking town. You think I don't know? I know everything and I'm going to tell her. I'm going to tell everybody."

A slap then. Hard and powerful. A scream, hers, follows.

"Tell everybody? You won't tell anybody shit. You won't even walk outta here."

"Bingo." Craig whispers.

"What the hell is—"

Then a gunshot. And two more. Then a fourth. And a final fifth.

No voices and my own is gone, scared into non-existence. My hands shake and my entire body is suddenly hot. Sweat everywhere, same as when I puke. I've known fear before but nothing like this.

This is overwhelming. Black and towering. Nerve-shattering.

A door at the far end of the hallway opens, closes. Someone walks toward us.

My hand goes to my gun but Craig stays it.

When I see her, I think for a moment it's *her*, Craig's her.

The woman passes us. Never looks. Never breathes.

Never wipes the blood from her face. Also on her shirt. A mechanic-style shirt, name tag over her left breast.

"—la," it says.

Then she's on the elevator and gone, the clank and clang eventually leaving us in silence.

Going into the loft, I notice the door. Bashed all to hell around the handle. Dented and bruised, battered out of shape. Inside, where I'd never been, Hubby is dead. Rose blossoms on his chest, holes in his head, one in his groin.

"He had girlfriends," Craig says. "Lots of them. I found Lola first."

"The phone calls," I say. "You amped her up. Told her all those things."

Craig nods. "He deserves it."

"Were any of them true?"

"All of them," Craig says. "Or none of them but others. Hubby was a piece of shit."

"No argument there."

"And now he's dead."

"Damn sure no argument there. Never seen anybody deader."

"Must'a broken in and found the owner," Craig says. "You see the door?"

"Or was waiting for a woman who hasn't lived here in months and the new owner found him. Killed an intruder."

Craig nods. "Maybe." Keys up his shoulder mic. "Dispatch from 312. Got a DB. Shooting. Better get me a dick or two."

I take a deep breath. Maybe we hadn't stepped in the shitty gutter as badly as I thought. Maybe we'd stepped lightly... which only meant the smell would permeate our souls.

"Detectives are going to figure it out pretty quickly."

Craig shakes his head. "Dicks won't care. An abandoned loft. Who knows what went on in here."

"Look at this," I say. In the kitchen. Window overlooks the street fifteen stories below. I can see the moon above.

Hubby splattered the window when he was being shot. The blood covered then dripped then diffused. Everything, seen through that window, is sheened in red and pink.

Including the moon.

No Outlet
David Housewright

Burroughs watched the black Acura turn onto the street and drive right up to the red and white striped traffic barrier preventing cars from falling into the ditch bordering the railroad tracks and he thought; did you not see the sign? Or did you not know what it meant? Back in the day, the black and yellow diamond-shaped sign read "Dead End" and everyone understood its meaning. Yet it had been recently replaced by the less alarming "No Outlet" and confusion reigned.

He thought better of the driver when he made his Y-turn, drove up the street, and parked in the metered space just beyond where Burroughs was sitting.

"Probably stopping for a beer," he told himself.

There was nothing else on the street that would interest an outsider. The business park at the end of the block had been shuttered for years. There was duplex dueling a four-plex across the street for the title of most dilapidated on one side of Riley's, and an ancient apartment building with a sign in front advertising vacancies on the other. The driver didn't seem interested in the bar, though. He left the Acura and walked to the bottom of the concrete steps where Burroughs was sitting.

"How you doin'?" the driver said.

"S'up?"

The driver gazed up at the building. It had once been a small warehouse someone had attempted to turn into artist lofts. There was a "For Rent" sign on its front door as well.

"I used to live here," he said.

"Oh yeah?"

"Third floor front. Had a nice view of Riley's if you wanna

call that a view."

"I live there now."

"Burroughs, right?"

"How did you—what's it to you?"

"Nothin'. Nothin' at all. I'm Kelly, by the way."

"Come 'ere sight-seein'? Gonna reminisce 'bout old times?"

"Naw, naw, man. When I left here, I promised myself I'd never come back."

"Then why didja?"

"You got a lot of hostility there, Burroughs. What's that about?"

"If yer lookin' for somethin' you left behind, talk to the building manager. When I took over the loft it was empty."

"Anything I wanted to keep, I took with me—which wasn't much, believe me."

"Then what you want?"

"Well, I'll tell ya, since you asked so nice. I'm looking for my mail."

"Mail? What, you didn't leave no forwarding address?"

"I did. Went to the post office and filled out the little card. This piece, though—it musta snuck through."

"I don't know anything about it."

"Now, now, think before you say. See, it was a very special piece of mail. Very important to me."

"Don't mean it's important to me."

"I'll make it worth your while, you help me out."

"You offerin' a reward or somethin'?"

"Somethin', yeah."

"Look, I don't know nuthin' 'bout your mail. Why don't you go talk to the person who sent it?"

"I did. Talked to him at great length. He said he took it to the post office, made sure it had the correct postage, dropped it in the box."

"Could be he's lying."

"No, no—I believe him. What they say, the truth will set you free? I kept tellin' him, truth will set you free, man, truth will set you free and he kept sayin' he put it in the mail, swear to God. So, yeah, I believe him. That's why I come lookin',

Burroughs. Why I come here. Sure you can't help me out?"

"I never saw no box."

"I didn't say it was a box."

"You musta."

"Don't think so, but—you know what? It was a box that was sent to me. You remember, now?"

"No. What I mean is—look, I got a box, but there was—your name is Kelly? There was no name on this box. And somethin' else, okay? It had the wrong address. 107 Third Street. This is 127 Third Street. So, what I did, I wrote on the box 'wrong address, return to sender' and left it for the mailman. That's what I did."

"Yeah, yeah, that's cool. I'd do the same. Except, the box was never returned to sender."

"That's not my fault."

"Did I say it was your fault?"

"I gave the box to the postman and he took it away. That's the truth. A couple days later..."

"What?"

"It came back. So what I did, I took it down the street. I was lookin' out for you, man. I took it down the street lookin' for the correct address, took it down to the office park thinkin' maybe it reopened, maybe there's someone conducting business there, you know? Only the place, it's still closed up. And the address—there is no 107 on this side of Third Street or t'other."

"So, what did you do?"

"I took it to the post office myself and I gave it to the guy and I said, I told 'em they fucked up. That there was no 107 Third Street and they should take care of this. And, and that's how I left it."

"Are you sure that's what you did?"

"You callin' me a liar? Is that what you're doin'?"

"You're a musician, aren't you Burroughs? How's that workin' out?"

"It's workin' out just fine."

"Bet it is, bet it is. I knew a guy is all. Had his own band. Loved it, he loved it, and he was good, too. But you know, it's a tough way to make a living 'specially when you're just startin' out, startin' to build an audience, startin' to build a rep. And the expense, man. Instruments. Amplifiers. Sound boards and shit. Easy t' see how a guy might give in to temptation."

"What do you mean?"

"You didn't open my box, did you? You didn't take what was inside."

"Fuck no."

"That's cool, that's cool. Except, you see, a guy like me's not all that different from a guy like you. Gotta build that rep and keep it. Make sure the people—your audience—make sure they know what to expect and then give it to 'em every time. Can't have no lapses otherwise—people they won't take you seriously, is what I'm sayin'. Gigs, they get harder and harder to come by."

"You don't know nuthin' 'bout the life."

"I know you can't be strummin' no lead guitar without fingers. But, hey, I've taken up too much of your time as it is. What I'm gonna do now, I'm goin' across the street and have a cold one. Talk to old man Riley. He still runnin' the place? And that barmaid, the one with the orange hair and big tits. What'shername? Eleanor. She was always one with the gossip. Always knew everything goin' on in the neighborhood. Whose marriages were in trouble, who was outta work, who just came into some money..."

"Wait, wait now, Kelly. I feel bad about this. I feel bad about you losin' your—mail. I kinda feel like it's my fault cuz I didn't do more to get it to its rightful owner. It wasn't my fault..."

"I understand."

"I just feel bad about it. And I can see—you've been a good guy 'bout all this—but I can see how you might hold me responsible."

"I'm just askin' that you look at it from my point of view."

"It's what I'm doin."

"So, what are you suggestin'?"

"I'm just wondering—is there any way we can work this out, you know, amicably?"

"Bet there is, bet there is."

Perko's Farm
Rob Brunet

Perko Ratwick needed a change in plans like he needed hemorrhoids. He rocked his Harley onto its kickstand and walked to the water's edge where a man stood fishing.

"Biting today?" he asked.

The man grunted and looked at the white bucket beside him. Perko peeked in and saw what had to be half a dozen scaly creatures, gills flapping on the top ones.

"These good eating?" Making conversation when he'd much rather knee-cap the fisherman. Four months of planning, a twenty-thousand-dollar down payment so this bugger could set up a suburban grow op, and now he calls to say the deal's off? No explanation?

"Free food." The man finished reeling in his line, shook a clump of weeds from its green and yellow lure, and cast again.

Perko didn't get it. Nghiem had to be worth a couple million, maybe more. He'd arrived from Vietnam a decade ago and was running at least six grow houses in the suburbs north of Toronto, one of which was supposed to supply Perko. Surely he could afford dinner. "We coulda met in a restaurant," said the biker. "I'd a picked up the tab."

Nghiem said, "Sense of obligation. No need."

"So what's the deal? Your message said something changed."

"No deal."

"Then what?"

"I said no deal. Go find new grower."

Perko said, "I don't understand. You're saying—"

"What so hard? NO GROW FOR YOU."

Perko watched as he tugged and reeled, pulling the lure through the shallows. Nghiem's plain white van sat forty feet away, backed in off the road. With cars passing every minute or so, there was no way to drag him over without being seen. Besides, chances were the guy had a couple goons inside the van in case their boss needed help delivering bad news.

"I've already lined up the sale," Perko said.

Nghiem's rod bent suddenly. He let a little line run out then started reeling again, still smooth and slow. "Cops busted two houses. One guy third time. He's not coming out soon."

The Vietnamese grower ran a straightforward game. Buy a nondescript house on a quiet street, grow three or four cycles of skunk weed. Fresh coat of paint, and sell the house to some sucker who wouldn't know it was full of mold until long after the check had cleared. Toughest part of the guy's operation was finding people fool enough to live in the houses while tending the plants, yet straight enough to fit in.

"What happened," Perko asked.

"Neighbors."

"They get nosey?"

"Kid got lonely. Had a barbecue."

"You gotta be kidding."

"Cost me crop, both houses. Now I have to pay lawyers."

"Fucking lawyers."

The Vietnamese sighed. "They are the breaks."

"Them," said Perko. "Them's the breaks."

"Yes."

"Problem is, my down payment."

"House is a crime scene. No can sell. Have to wait."

"Waiting ain't my specialty."

"I pay. Five thousand a week. You have in no time."

"I'd rather the weed. We had a deal."

"Your money." Nghiem nudged the white bucket with his foot. "Take it."

"There'll be interest."

"See you next week. No problem?" The man grinned, mouth full of yellow teeth. Perko imagined yanking them one by one with a set of pliers. Nghiem glanced over his shoulder to the white van. No question he had backup. His rod bent double, and he started reeling fast. Perko looked at the dying fish piled on top of one another. He tilted the bucket on its side to reveal a sliver of pink plastic bag. Pinching it between his thumb and two fingers, he tugged. As it pulled free, two fish started flopping, slapping his forearm, making it slick with slime.

He walked back to his bike and wiped his hands and the bag in the grass. He watched Nghiem land a rock bass, bang its head against the ground, and drop it in the bucket. Driving away, Perko was relieved to find the fish smell disappeared in the wind.

Bad enough Nghiem's screw-up messed with Perko Ratwick's plans to move a few hundred kilos of high grade pot. Business was business and the biker had talked his way out of worse corners before. The New York buyers would still be there once he found a new supply. It wasn't about one deal, though. Perko had a real shot at making Road Captain in the Libidos Motorcycle Club. Launch himself into the big leagues—a guy who brokered deals between rival gangs and lined the Libidos coffers without taking on real exposure. Kind of like an investment banker, only quicker. And less paperwork.

He set a meet with a guy named Frederick who wanted into the Libidos in a bad way.

"Maybe it's a good thing the gook fell through," Perko said.

"How dat."

"Maybe I been coming at this wrong."

The men were sitting at a picnic table in dead quiet downtown Bobcaygeon. The ice had barely broken up and the locks wouldn't be operational for a few weeks yet. Perko said, "These locks run, what, five months a year?"

"'Bout dat," said Frederick.

"And when they do, they're only open something like eight, ten hours a day?"

"So?"

"So, the water never stops flowing."

"No?"

"'Course not," said Perko. "They control the water level, but they don't kill the flow."

Frederick looked from the locks to Perko and said, "What you mean?"

"Do I gotta paint the whole picture? Instead of waitin' for some other guy to deliver supply, I could be growin' myself. Year-round. Much as I like."

"So you take on more risk."

"Not if I do things right. Arm's length," Perko said. "That's where you come in."

"How come me?"

"You wanna patch Libido some day? Earn your stripes. Couple things I need you to do."

Frederick nodded slowly.

"First, find me a grower," Perko said. "Make sure he's no fool."

"And the other thing?"

"It's a little more complicated," Perko said, and told him about Nghiem's rate of pay.

Perko decided to go all pro. Thinking about Nghiem's lonely grower and the barbecue, he wasn't about to put his own name on the deed for some suburban shack on a street full of busybodies. Besides, once he got the gig going, he'd need two houses, then four. Before he knew it, he'd be back begging product from the fish-frying bastard. Never mind how many growers he'd wind up hiring. The more he thought about it, the less his plan felt risk-free. The Libidos would let him run with it, take their cut, but his ass would be hanging way out there. No, what Perko needed was a large-scale operation. Leverage.

He found a farm.

Mildred Perrigrew owned the farm and had lived on it for nearly sixty-five years, starting when she married Orvus Perrigrew the week she graduated from Grade Ten. Orvus was twenty-two at the time and had only stayed in school himself until Grade Six, dropping out to work the farm with his uncle until the elder Perrigrew passed away. When Orvus inherited the land, he immediately looked around for a mate. Marrying Mildred was a real coup: he got himself a young wife as well as a capable bookkeeper, since Mildred had taken both accounting and typing classes for the two years she was in high school.

All of this Perko Ratwick learned from Mildred herself when he responded to her ad in the *Peterborough Examiner*:

FARM FOR RENT
Good barn. Better house. Not much of a woodlot,
but good water and some apple trees.
$3,000 monthly. Cash only.
Contact Mildred at Hillview Retirement
Residence, Peterborough.

Perko tried telephoning, but the attendant said Mildred had left strict instructions that she intended to meet potential renters in person.

"You can tell a lot about a man from looking in his eyes, my daddy always told me," Mildred said to Perko over a cup of coffee in the Hillview sun room. "Did I already say 'Thank you' for the donuts? Well, thank you, kindly, anyway. What a nice young man you are." Perko had brought a dozen Krispy Kremes. Between the two of them, he and Mildred had already eaten half the box.

"I gave Orvus four children, don't you know," Mildred said. "Two girls and two boys, before I lost Orvus during childbirth." She paused and watched Perko pick up flakes of dried honey from the table top with his fingertip. She gave a little shrug and continued: "It happened when I went into labor with Jeremy. Orvus sent our eldest, Marianne, to fetch the doctor. Doc Grainger lived about five miles up the main road. Marianne was only nine at the time, but we were used to trusting her with important errands. She was pretty independent and knew how to handle a horse."

"Right. So, do I gotta give the rent money to this Marianne or to you?" Perko asked, scratching his chin.

"To me, young man. It's my farm, not the children's." She squinted at him and stuck out her lower lip. "Now, where was I? Oh, yes. I told Orvus, go get some hot water and clean towels. And step on it, I said, 'cause you know that number four is like as not to come along even faster than number three did. So Orvus tells Baxter—he was six, no, seven years old—to build a fire in the woodstove. Baxter ran straight out to the woodshed to get some logs. Then, don't you know it, Greta—she was barely two and a half—well she decides she wants a bottle, and she started to cry.

"'Don't you be worried about me, Orvus Perrigrew,' I told him. 'You just give Greta her bottle and then come back with some water for me to drink. The doctor will be here soon enough. Besides, it isn't as if I'm new to childbearing.'

"So off he goes and leaves me in the bedroom, and Greta follows him out to the kitchen. There was a jug of milk left from breakfast because I always made sure we kept enough for the afternoon. I guess Orvus must have been pouring the milk into a saucepan to heat it on the stove, because I heard Greta get all excited. I figure she was hanging on his pant leg the way she liked to do some times, because I heard Orvus say, 'No sweetheart. We can't play airplane right now. Poppy's got to take care of Mommy.'

"The next thing I hear is Baxter shouting out as he stomped back in the kitchen: 'Here's the wood, Poppy.' I figure the door must have struck Orvus on the backside because, well, Baxter told me later, Orvus just spun around, with Greta hanging onto his pants for dear life. I heard her shrieking, but it was for joy, you know, the way babies do. Baxter stumbled and I heard the logs he was carrying spill onto the kitchen floor. Baxter told me Orvus's feet flew out from under him when he stepped on one of the rolling logs. He landed flat on his back. That was one very loud crash, mercy me. I jumped right out of the bed, labor or no labor, and walked across the bedroom so I could see into the kitchen. The saucepan had flown out of Orvus's hands and clattered down beside him. There was milk everywhere. Greta was bouncing up and down on Orvus's belly and shrieking, 'Again, Poppy! Again! Do fly-fly again!'

"Orvus wasn't moving and I figured he must have smacked his head on the corner of the stove."

"So, was he dead?"

"Dead? Dear me, no! It would take more than a knock on the noggin to do in Orvus Perrigrew. He was fine stock, my husband." Mildred reached for another donut, took one bite and then licked her fingers as she passed it back and forth between her hands. Perko sighed and scraped some dirt from under his thumbnail.

"After just a moment or two, Orvus's eyes fluttered open and he said, 'I better get some more milk.'

"Well, it was early in the day to be milking a cow for the second time, but Orvus wasn't about to leave his baby girl without her bottle, so he picked up the milk jug and headed out to the barn. And that's the very last I saw of him."

"So he just took off on you? Left you with the kids? End of story?" Perko asked, trying not to sound too hopeful.

"Of course not! What a silly question. He would never do such a thing. Besides, like I told you, Orvus *died* during childbirth." She paused to eat half the donut. Perko grabbed one himself and shoved it whole into his mouth, pushing the last bit in with his thumb and wiping his fingers on his jeans.

"See, I got the pains again right after he left the house and so I made my way back to the bedroom. Baxter did his best to take care of me, and Marianne arrived with Doc Grainger soon enough. No one even noticed Orvus was missing until after Jeremy was born, cleaned up, and in my arms. Except Greta, of course, but her crying didn't get a whole lot of attention once my pains began in earnest, and I was making all my own noises and such.

"Then Doc Grainger said to Baxter to go get his pa so he could meet his new son, and Baxter went out and came back white as a ghost two minutes later. He said, 'Poppy's under Bessie'—she was our cow—'and he don't look too good at all and he's not talking or nothing.'

"Seems somehow Orvus must have tripped up Bessie while trying to milk her, or maybe she was real upset at getting milked a second time so early in the day. Whatever the case, Bessie's leg was broken and all fifteen hundred pounds of her were laying on top of Orvus. Baxter said he had an awful grimace frozen on his face. Like he knew he was done for when it happened—and just how much Bessie was worth to our family. But there isn't a whole lot a soul can do when a cow lands on you."

Mildred quietly finished her donut and licked the honey off her fingers once more. She fixed Perko Ratwick in the eye and said, "So that's how come I raised my children all alone on the farm. And maybe having to work so hard while they were growing up is why one by one they left the land as soon as a better opportunity came along—not that I blame them—and now I'm just too old to live out there but still I can't bring myself to sell it because, well, you know, you just never know, do you. Maybe one of the grandkids will want to revive the farm. Or maybe they'll just sell it once I'm in the ground, but that will be the kids' decision, not mine. Now, what did you say you wanted to do out there, Mr. Smith?"

Perko shoved the last donut into his mouth, took a gulp of coffee and resumed staring at Mildred with his best attempt at an interested look. Half a minute passed before it dawned on him that the old biddy had stopped talking.

"Mr. Smith? I say, why is it you want to rent my farm?"

"I'm a... ahem... a painter," he said. "I'm looking for a place where I can get close to nature. I especially like plants." He paused and blinked slowly. Mildred stared at him like he was speaking in a foreign tongue. "Some of my canvases are really big, so I figure I'll set up my operation in your barn."

Mildred continued to stare. She asked, "Couldn't you just rent an apartment or something? What do you need with a farm?"

"It's real important to me to find peace and quiet. Money's no object where my creativity is concerned."

"You do realize the hayfields have already been rented to the neighbor."

"I just need the barn."

"It comes with the house, too."

"Fine by me."

"I'd feel better if you had a look at it first. I don't want any landlord-tenant headaches at my age."

"No really, I—"

The look in Mildred's eye made Perko shut up and listen.

He couldn't remember the last time he'd been put in his place quite so firmly. She said, "Here's the key. You go have a look around and come back and tell me what you decide."

"I'll be back tomorrow," he said.

"I'm not going anywhere." She pushed herself to her feet and shuffled across the room to where a game of Snap was getting started. She gave him one last look, jerked her chin toward the door, and said, "Deal me in."

Perko sat in the bow of the fishing boat wearing a floppy hat bedecked with lures. Using the electric motor, Frederick navigated close to the rocky shore. The water was deep enough he could have used the outboard but a silent approach was critical. They got within twenty feet of Nghiem before he even realized he had company. He smiled, waved, and cast his line in the opposite direction. When he noticed the boat was nosing up against the causeway he warned them to watch out for the bottom. Even when Perko jumped in the knee deep water and scrambled across the zebra mussel-encrusted rock, it was clear the Vietnamese took him for just another fisherman until he got a good look at his face. By then it was too late. Perko clocked him with a paddle and Frederick leapt ashore to help drag him into the boat. Frederick insisted on snatching the white pail full of fish. It wasn't until he fired up the outboard and buzzed out onto the lake that there was any sign of movement from the white van facing the road. If Nghiem's bodyguards did fire their guns, they missed. Perko couldn't hear a damn thing over the two hundred twenty horsepower engine's roar.

Drifting in the middle of the lake, Perko prodded Nghiem with his foot and splashed water on his face. "Scream and I'll cut you some gills," Perko said.

The man just lay there on his side in the boat's hull, his eyes blinking like a bass.

"You're gonna make a phone call," Perko said. "My cash gets delivered, with a ten thousand kicker, before morning. All of it. If it don't, the rest of your houses are going down, and we'll find out how well you swim with your hands tied to your feet." Perko asked him what number to dial then held the phone to his ear.

Frederick baited a hook and dropped a line off starboard.

"Well, isn't this a pleasant surprise, Mr. Smith," Mildred said, flipping open the fresh box of Krispy Kremes.

Perko Ratwick remained standing. There were plenty more donuts where those came from, and he wasn't in the mood to hear about life—nor *death*—on the farm he was about to rent. "Everything checks out," he said. "I'll take it."

"Do sit, Mr. Smith. Tell me about your paintings."

He leaned in close and said quietly, "I noticed a little unconventional wiring in a couple of the outbuildings. Mind if I clean that up while I'm out there?"

She nibbled a donut and looked as though she hadn't heard.

"Mrs. Perrigrew, I'd like to rent your farm."

"Like the ad said, it'll be three thousand dollars a month, in cash, and I would very much like it if you brought a box of these donuts with you each time you come to pay me." Perko offered Mildred his hand and she shook it. "You know, you do smell rather like Orvus did. A real manly smell. Have you been fishing?"

Forcing a smile, Perko took a thick wad of bills out of his jacket pocket. Mildred's eyes sparkled wide when she saw the money, then narrowed again suddenly. "First and last month's rent, of course," she said.

Perko grinned and nodded. It wasn't like he'd be coming back any time soon.

"And did I mention that there would be a damage deposit? I can't very well be chasing after a young buck like you at my age, now can I?"

"Here's the first eight months' rent," he said, thumbing a stack of bills and laying them on the table. "And other five grand damage deposit."

Mildred's eyes darted left and right as she swept the money off the table and tucked it into a large pocket on the front of her frock. She seemed satisfied nobody had witnessed the transaction.

"Well, now, that's mighty thoughtful of you, Mr. Smith."

As Perko turned to leave, she said, "Mr. Smith, could you do me a favor?"

He forced his shoulders to relax and pasted what he hoped was a friendly smile on his face. "What?"

"On your way out, kindly tell that nice young man at the front desk I will be taking the bus to the Horned Owl Casino this evening, after all."

Shanko Has a Beer
Gary Phillips

Tal Shanko enjoyed the austere taste of the micro-brew called Black Hammer Ale. The beer menu of the Reserve micro-brewery and restaurant boasted some fifty different offerings. Not all of them were in-house libations, as some were obscure selections from around the world including names he couldn't pronounce from Thailand and Bosnia. The establishment was a converted old school diner and he'd gotten a seat at the counter. Over his left shoulder at a booth tucked mid-way down, sat a man and a woman, both in their twenties. They were appropriately dressed hipster cool for the area—she wore a snap brim hat and a small ring hung from below the man's mouth over his soul patch.

Shanko had driven down from Northern California. He figured it must have been when he stopped for lunch at Milburn's Tavern where he was tagged. That wasn't too hard for whoever was behind this to do. When he did make forays down south to L.A., three or four times a year, he usually stopped at a choice among three or four establishments for a late lunch off of 101. Predictability was vulnerability he admonished himself, that warning echoing from his DI back in Basic still true all these decades down the line. They would have a spotter stationed at each location, waiting for him to show then plant a GPS device on his beat-looking Ford pick-up that actually had a newly rebuilt hemi engine under the hood. Slipping. Another sign his rocking chair years were getting closer each day he reflected.

When he was driving through Thousand Oaks, he wondered if he was imagining the late model Audi in his rearview, hadn't it been steady on him for several miles? But traffic had been bunching up for some time due to a fender bender. There had been several of the same sort of cars trailing his vehicle. The Audi went away somewhere in the San Fernando Valley but Shanko relaxed only to a few degrees. He didn't take out his burner, his disposable cell, for fear the call could be intercepted. Intellectually he knew this wasn't very likely as the device didn't have internet access which made it easier for spy software to latch onto its signal, but the tried and true methods were called that for a reason so he'd stick with his intuition. Plus the old way gave him a chance to confirm his suspicions.

He'd gotten off the freeway and found a working pay phone at a nearby gas station and mini-mart. He made his call, scanning his surroundings as he did so. A light-colored Camry he thought he recognized drove past on the access road. The driver possibly suspecting they'd been made Shanko surmised. Whether it was the IRS, the ATF or another entity, they wouldn't be backing off. He got back on the road and eventually after sundown, wound his way to this micro-brew eatery in Silver Lake in L.A.

The couple had come in after him and initially they blended in with the other patrons. It was when the woman had gone to the restroom, a path taking her past him at the counter, that Shanko's alarm went off. She was shapely and wore hip hugger jeans and a loose T-shirt with a rock band's logo on its front. She might have a gun tucked snugly in her waistband but he couldn't tell. What he did notice was the two knuckles on her left hand as she passed near him. There were more pronounced like a prize fighter's or somebody who practiced mixed martial arts. Could be this had nothing to do with him, but he better find out. After all, he had equipment bags filled with eight million in cash secured in the false bottom of the pick-up's bed. That was plenty to get your head blown off about.

As much as he would have liked to finish his tasty brew, he knew he needed to stay sharp. He only had a third of his drink and finished off one half of a tuna melt sandwich.

"I'm sorry, you didn't enjoy your food or beer?" the pretty waitress with the expressive eyes said when she come over.

"It's not that, everything was fine," he smiled weakly,

patting his mid-section. "Stomach's a little upset is all."

"Well, hope you feel better," she said cheerily, taking his dinner away.

She returned with the bill and Shanko paid. He got up and went out to his truck on the parking lot. If the couple were bird-dogging him, they played it well. But then, assuming they had the benefit of electronic tracking, there had no need to tip their hand by hurrying. The restaurant was located on a triangle of land so that on one side you could exit the lot onto what became a residential street angling up a low rise. The other side let out onto lower Sunset and Shanko went this way, heading west into Hollywood. If it was the authorities behind him, they'd want to catch him in the process of making his money drop.

Shanko made his money as a marijuana grower in what was now termed the Emerald Triangle. Essentially these were hidden acreages of weed growing on public or private lands cultivated throughout Humboldt and Mendocino counties, with some overlap into Oregon. When the peaceniks and Panthers were doing their thing back in the day of afros and a fruging Ann-Margret, Shanko was on his second tour of duty in Vietnam as a tunnel rat. He was one of a select group of soldiers who'd managed, if they lived, to balance the sweating fear against the intoxicating exhilaration of inching their way along a VC tunnel, crawling at times under the earth for what might be several clicks along a barely shored up earthen worm hole in the dark. Where at any juncture, bamboo spikes or a round from Charlie would be the reward for your impertinence.

Heading to his destination, Shanko kept a lid on his apprehension. He knew the couple was out there nearby, shadowing his movements with their tracking device. Shanko hadn't made any effort to find it on his vehicle or remove the thing. He wanted answers, aware he was gambling his freedom against his curiosity. But the more he worked it over in his mind, the more he was convinced these were civilians and not the law. He was wound like that time in the tunnel they'd found on the outskirts of Cu Chi and he'd been sent down.

He'd gone about four hundred yards, stooping lower as he went because the ceiling sloped down, telescoping in so much it even got tight for the compact GI. Then he had the sudden impression there was a presence ahead. Most likely he calculated from experience there was one or more of the enemy in a fork off the main tunnel he was in. They too must have sensed his presence and had gone stone. He laid flat, his confiscated Makarov Soviet made pistol in one hand with a canister of CS gas around his neck on a thin cord to be easily ripped free. The tunnel rats preferred using the smaller caliber Makarovs as the Army-issued .45 was too loud and gave off too much flash in such confined spaces.

But those goddamn fire ants were about too. Like a horror version of *Gulliver's Travels*, those insectoid Lilliputians crawled all over him. Their pincers jabbed at the flesh of his arms, chest and face causing hot stings of pain repeatedly. But he couldn't cry out and swat at them as that might have made too much noise. So he waited silently, teeth gritted, doing what he could to keep his mind empty of anything else but surviving.

Past Western and the twenty-four hour Home Depot, Shanko neared the 101 Freeway and crossing the overpass, soon took a narrow street off Sunset to the right. Down that block with featureless apartment buildings side-by-side, he turned into a driveway that took him to a carport area behind one of the nondescripts. He didn't park in a slot but in the alleyway itself, blocking cars in their assigned stalls. He got out and two other vehicles, each from the opposite direction, entered the alley, headlights defining his form. The couple got out of a Jeep Liberty, the man aiming a Remington semi-auto shotgun at Shanko, who raised his hands. Behind him a lone man, a muscular Latino with tattoos and a clean shaven head, had exited a street racer tricked out Nissan 240SX. He held a handgun on the marijuana grower.

"Get the money out," the woman ordered Shanko.

"Who you working for?"

"I'll text you later with an answer," she cracked. "Get to getting', home slice."

Shanko lowered his hands. "I think we can discuss it

now." As he said this, a red dot appeared on the woman's forehead. Laser sighting dots popped up on the other two as well. From windows in an apartment building opposite of where they stood, it seemed unseen snipers had them in their crosshairs

"I can assure you they have night scopes and will cut you down if you twitch," Shanko said.

"Excellent," the one with the tats enthused. He put his gun on the hood of his car.

The other two exchanged grins and the man put the shotgun on the ground. He beamed broadly at Shanko. "You do your reputation proud, sir."

"Indeed, indeed," the larger man echoed, joining the couple.

"Are you guys high?" Shanko said, picking up the pistol, and putting his foot on the shotgun.

"High on you, brother," the woman beamed.

Her companion with the soul patch nodded upward. "Can we talk someplace?"

"I don't get you three."

"You will," the muscular one said. "Our weapons were just for show."

Shanko released the magazine in the handgun. It was empty as was its chamber. He put the gun in his back pocket and checking the shotgun, confirmed it too was empty. By then, another man appeared along the walkway of the apartment building where the supposed assortment of snipers were. This man, in his mid-sixties, balding and pot-bellied, had a genial thick mustachioed face. He wore khakis and a colorful print shirt over his waistband. There was a .45 at his side. Upstairs, he'd trained the laser pointers on the trio, creating the impression there were more than just him with rifles.

"What the hell's going on, Tal?"

"Damned if I know, Mish, but we're gonna find out."

"I'll move the cars," the tatted one offered happily.

"You do that, snowflake," Tom "Mish for Mission" Alward said. "I'll keep an eye on you while your buddies go upstairs with Tal." He produced a Beretta from under his shirt and handed it over to Shanko.

"Come on," Shanko said. He pointed down a walkway with the gun and the two preceded him to an apartment on the third floor of the three-story building. It was furnished functionally and Shanko directed the couple to sit together on a couch.

"Guess we'll wait for Hector to come back with your friend," the woman said, "before we lay it out."

"I guess so," Shanko said, curious but showing a blank face. Soon the other two men were inside as well.

"Let's get to it," Shanko said once the one called Hector was also crowded on the couch.

"We took over my Uncle Ned's farm," the young woman began. "He retired to Detroit."

"Detroit?" Alward blurted. "Why the hell would anyone retire there?"

"It's going green fields and property is cheap," she replied.

Shanko knew Ned Vankin. He was an ex-hippie, back to the land type who'd come to the Emerald Triangle years before the area was called that. He'd gotten into growing weed at volume for Zen reasons. He was the last of his kind. These days marijuana was big business and big risks.

He frowned. "You're Carlye?"

"Yep." She pointed at the muscular one, "That's Hector and he's Ric," indicating the man with the soul patch.

He turned to Alward. "These kids are all right, man. Break out some refreshments, will you?"

"Sure, Mr. Benny." Alward cracked, tucking his gun away. He went to a cupboard to retrieve a bottle of scotch and some plastic cups. This was a crash place Shanko kept among several others in the Southland.

Shanko addressed Carlye Vankin. "I haven't seen you since you were what? Twelve?"

"She's all growed up now," Alward observed as he set down the cups and bottle on a chair he'd brought over. There were no tables.

"Why all the rigmarole, Carlye?" Shanko asked.

"We wanted to show you were capable," soul patch remarked.

"That we had game," the muscled one added. He'd moved to a nearby chair.

Shanko looked from Alward back to them. "Game for what?"

"To go up against the cartel," Vankin said solemnly.

Shanko said, "They've been nosing around?"

"There's a slick one, a Chicano who calls himself Lukas L'Amour," Hector Garagos huffed. "He's a representative of the Del Sol Cartel."

"I've heard of them," Shanko acknowledged. Not as large or as influential as Los Zetas or the Gulf Cartel, the Del Sol combine nonetheless had its own nasty reputation including disemboweling bloggers who dared to report drug crime atrocities using social media. The narco-traffickers liked to be extolled, not vilified.

"He showed up one day and told us either they get a cut or we're through," Vankin said. "We didn't agree to anything but a week or so later we could see the evidence of an attack of a mycoherbicide on our plants."

"You sure this wasn't coincidental? Growers always have fungus problems," Alward stated.

"He left some canisters around so we would know it was him," Ric Deen replied. "Then two of our harvesters were jumped and beaten pretty badly in town. One guy lost an eye."

"We didn't come to you to whine, Tal," Vankin emphasized. "This is about us taking a stand against these bastards. It's not like the cartels haven't made moves in the past into the Triangle."

Shanko was standing, hands on his hips. "You're right. But usually they send in a crew they've contracted, maybe one of their men supervising and work their own acreage, widen their patches, then muscle others out."

"The small ones who don't have soldiers like you, man," Deen said.

Shanko said to Vankin, "This could be an opening salvo. Crowd in the smaller growers to eventually put a ring around the bigger farms." He looked off into the near distance then re-focused. "I'll make some inquiries."

"Inquiries?" Hector Garagos blared, leaning forward. "Shit. We didn't come down here and go through all this to have you ask around." He slapped the back of one hand into the palm of the other more than once. "We need to put it to these *pendejos* like hard and now, home. Carlye said you was a sure enough hope to die nail their balls to the wall motherfucker. Inquiries? What the fuck, huh?"

Alward looked bemused. "Wish I was young again."

Shanko repeated evenly, "I'll make a few inquiries."

Garagos glared at him open-mouthed.

Lukas L'Amour entered the clearing flanked by two gunners handling compact but lethally efficient Beretta PM 12-S assault rifles on shoulder tethers. Around them in the still warm air grew maturing marijuana stalks some eight feet or more high. The three stood looking at the drying barn used by Carlye Vankin and her partners on the pot farm her hippie relatives began decades ago. The farm was located in the hills overlooking the town of Northpitch, some seventy miles or so west of Redding in Northern California.

"Come on," L'Amour said and started walking, a confident sneer on his handsome face.

The first round from the rifle equipped with a suppressor on the end of its barrel put the first gunner down with a hit to his chest. This time there was no pretending. This time there had been the opportunity to prepare.

The second armed man reacted quickly and raked a burst from his weapon across the marijuana stalks. Clumps of the plant, sticky with their potent resin, swirled about in the air. This one also went over after two more rounds cut into his upper body. L'Amour was reaching for the fallen hood's assault rifle but stopped at the sound of Tal Shanko's voice near him.

"Leave it alone," he said.

L'Amour straightened. "Who the hell are you?"

"What matters is you listening to me. I know you've been looking for a way into the Del Sol cartel and you figured what better way than showing them you could be the one to deliver profits from out of here to them. Not a bad idea, really," he admitted. "But it's not going to happen, not with you at least."

"So you say," L'Amour replied calmly.

"The third one is dead, too," Shanko said, referring to the armed lookout the gangster entrepreneur had placed among the plants some yards deep. Shanko and Alward had done recon. One more body to be disposed of out here. One more body to fertilize the crops.

The confident look returned to L'Amour's face and Shanko reacted. He ran and dove into the stalks as more gunfire, single shots, erupted. There was a fourth gunner, this one high up in one of the oak trees, their foliage used to help camouflage the marijuana plants from DEA helicopters.

"What you got to say now, grandpa?" L'Amour taunted, a handgun in his grip. He also entered the stalks figuring to hunt Shanko by the sound of his movement and not be a target for the other man's shooters. Though he had the impression there was only one other and he hoped his man would spot both from up above. L'Amour moved through the growth, gun extended. To his left was a sound and he turned and fired. Nothing. He stopped and listened, regretting he didn't have a way to communicate with his sniper but what difference would that make? Was there visibility into the grow area?

Speculation was useless, L'Amour reasoned, regaining control was paramount. Behind him there was movement and turning and shooting, he could hear thrashing about and saw plants shaking. He followed this and came to a path between rows of plantings. He looked about, aware it was too damn quiet.

"Hey, I think I know who you are, ese. Shanko, right? You were friends with the girl's uncle. Yeah, that's right, I've done my homework. I got this on lock, old man. It won't be long before I gank your shit, too."

To his right and behind him there was sound and he readied himself, wary for an attack. He headed back into the stalks when he stepped past a plot of ground. A plywood lid under earth and leaves over it flopped open, and an arm lashed out from the recently dug spider hole. The hand at the end of the arm grabbed the surprised man by an ankle. L'Amour didn't get a chance to shoot as he went down in the dirt on his chin, stunned. He also didn't get a chance to clear the whirling in his head before Shanko was on his back, a hand chop to his carotid artery causing his eyes to lose focus.

Shanko, breathing harder than he liked, stood, the gun in his hand. He blinked rapidly, shaking off a flashback in that tunnel in Cu Chi. The CS gas chocking his lungs, the ant welts covering his body, a knife wound bleeding profusely as two-handed, he drove the enemy's head onto a bamboo spike.

Carlye Vankin and Mish Alward stood near him as well. Alward was sweating heavily.

"You either tell your man to come down or I put one in you," Shanko said. "Then we get him anyway."

L'Amour stared at him. He had no doubt Shanko would shoot him in cold blood. From what he heard about the older man, he'd set you on fire then toss you gas soaked rags to put it out. What worried him was what would come after he did as he was told. Maybe a bullet now would be better than on the run once it was known he'd pimped the Del Sol's name like he was one of them. Those locos might not appreciate his enterprising spirit. L'Amour called out.

Tal Shanko was in his second-story office overlooking the Taj Mahal hotel in Northpitch. The main building, including the reflecting pool, was modeled on the original in Agra, India. Off this were cottages done in a similar style. Weed money had built the hotel and accounted for various McMansions about town. As Shanko had fallen into the growing business some decades ago, he now found himself as developer and investor in the town and in other projects elsewhere.

L'Amour hadn't been the real deal but one day there might be an actual encroachment from one of the cartels. The days of the notion that farming marijuana was a victimless crime were gone and he and the other growers in their loose association knew this. Nor was it like the authorities weren't getting more sophisticated in their tech and tenacity in ferreting out the plants and tracking the money trail. Carlye Vankin and her crew might like to believe otherwise, hyped on getting back to nature and living off the grid, but time was getting tight. Better then to step up diversifying their profits to be ready for the inevitable.

"Yeah, Jeff," he said into the burner he was using. "I'd like to see about putting some funds into the microbrewery industry. Uh-huh," he said, listening. "Great, see what you can find out and let me know. All right, cool, man."

Shanko hung up. Standing at the window, he looked out onto the lush hills, a map of where his hidden acreages were in those hills imprinted on his mind. Overhead a light plane buzzed that might be civilians or yet another pass by the authorities with their heat seeking scanners. Yeah, getting out of this crazy business, maybe going full hog into the microbrewery thing was looking good to Shanko. Legal vice. He checked his watch. Time for happy hour and a beer.

The Mor Doo's Revenge
Tom Crowley

"I'm all in." With those words, Nok proclaimed both her faith in her hand and her faith in her good fortune. She pushed all the chips she had left into the middle of the table. Then she sat back and fingered the good fortune amulet hanging around her neck. Rubbing it for its magic.

Jack, squinted at her across the table and then slowly, confidently pushed across a stack of chips to match her bet.

"Well, it took all night but it seems the girl's developed a set of balls."

The other players—only two others left from the group of eight starting twelve hours ago—sat back to see how the night would end. The curtains to Jack's Pool Bar were closed, but the morning sun was peeking around the edges highlighting the dirty floor and drab walls never meant to see the light of day.

"Not yet, but I'll be able to buy a set of balls after this hand if I want. Have a look."

Nok laid down her two hole cards, two kings, matching up nicely with the king and two eights displayed on the table.

"Huh, you don't need to buy a set of balls darling, just buy yourself some bigger tits. They'll pay for themselves in a month."

Jack threw down his hole cards, "But not today, young thing. Take a look at my red colors, all hearts, darling, and in order six through ten. Time to go home."

"Aiiyah, the gods have deserted me. Shit!" Nok was white faced with shock. This couldn't be happening. She'd been promised. The Mor Doo, the most famous fortune teller in Bangkok, a former monk famed for being in touch with the powers of the supernatural, had read her fortune. She had the sacred amulet. It was guaranteed. Good fortune was hers.

She clutched at the amulet hanging from her neck. He had blessed this. Why had it failed?

Nok was in trouble, big trouble. She had borrowed the money to buy into the game. The loan was due yesterday. She was so sure she would win. She had been promised.

"Next time, kid. The cards will treat you better."

"Jack, this cleans me out. Could I borrow some taxi money?"

"Sure, kid. Here's five hundred baht. Pay me back next time."

She stumbled away from the table towards the door, the world reeling around her.

"Thanks, Jack. I'll be back."

Earlier that evening, Matt Chance walked down the narrow soi towards the entrance to Jack's Pool Bar. Near the end of the soi, on one side just a few feet in front of the bar entrance, stood the spirit house on a stand five feet high. Nearly all buildings in Thailand, no matter how modest a home or grand an office building, have a spirit house erected on a front corner of the property. Most often these are miniature stick homes holding miniature figurines accompanied by a small statue of the Buddha or a Hindu god. It is believed good fortune follows erecting such a shrine and placing daily offerings of food and flowers to the gods. The buildings on either side of the soi blocked the setting sun and the walkway was wreathed in shadows. Matt saw movement in the shadow over the spirit house but could not make out what it was. As he walked closer, he saw that a large rat had climbed to the spirit house and was feeding on the fruit offering. Matt slowed his pace not wanting to get within leaping distance of the rat as it sensed his presence. The rat turned and darted off the stand to the ground and disappeared into a drainpipe running alongside the building.

Matt could only shake his head. It was a sign of the state of things in his life. He was strung tight. It had been six months since he had left the army. His physical wounds from combat in Afghanistan were healed. However his psyche was still very much on the mend. The army doctors talked about the need for treatment for post-traumatic stress. For Matt and his battle buddies, it boiled down to dealing with the anger and knowledge of being betrayed by a political military system that had used them. He hadn't come to terms with his anger, yet. Since he had left the states to return to his mother's home city of Bangkok his self-prescribed therapy sessions consisted of a few hours of play on the pool table on an almost daily basis. He found the need to focus on the green felt and the click and run of the ivory balls eased his mind better than anything. Well, better than anything except booze and he was determined to cut back on that.

As he approached the glass doors to the pool bar they swung open and Da, one of Matt's usual pool partners, was there to greet him.

"Hey, Matt. Good to see you."

"Hey, Da. Got time for a few games?"

Da was ten percent owner of the bar so she was on the scene most of the time. She was one of the best women players and Matt could usually count on her to give him a good game. She was what the Thai called a "tom," a woman who took the male role in a lesbian relationship. It confused some western visitors as Da was a Jodie Foster look-alike, an attractive face with a bit of an angular chin, narrow lips and penetrating eyes. She was five-foot eight inches tall, slim not skinny. She wore her hair short and spiked as was the current gay fashion and had four small diamonds in the lobe of her left ear. The only other telltale was she had a bit of an attitude. Matt found that more attractive. He liked women with attitude, lesbian or not. Da was in her early thirties and functioned as an older sister to many of the young Thai girls coming in the bar.

"I'm sorry, not today, Matt."

Then she caught Matt by the arm as he walked through the door and pulled him to the side for a quiet word amidst the rock music background throbbing through the bar.

"Actually it would help me if you could play some games with Nok." She pointed to an attractive girl dressed in black slacks and a loose white blouse sitting in one of the booths on the side intent on slurping up some noodles. She had long legs and long black hair which flowed down her back in the country girl style. "You know her, she shoots a pretty good game. She's got some problems right now and if you could play with her it would help relax her before the card game tonight."

"Okay. I'm not sure how good a game I'm shooting right now anyway. Anything special going on?"

"No just the usual. She's borrowed too much money and is counting to make it back big in the game tonight. You know that's the worst way to go into a game."

"Actually I don't know. I've got no interest in betting on the cards."

Da paused a moment and then continued, the big sister in her coming out.

"All these girls start out at sixteen or seventeen in the sex trade and have a hard time pulling themselves out. Nok chose this route: drugs, mostly speed, drinking, going twenty-four hours a day to burn herself out. Then her dad died, her mom got sick and this last year she has really fought back trying to get hold of herself. No more drugs, no more booze, trying to save enough to take care of her mom who has cancer. She gambles too much and loses too much, but she has nowhere else to turn. I can't stop her from the game. I've nothing else to offer her.

"She's a good kid, Matt. She never makes trouble. She looks out for the other girls. She's doing the best that she can. Just play a few sets with her and help her to relax and get her mind off of things. Maybe that will help her later."

"No problem, Da." Matt laughed, "Maybe playing with her will help me get my mind off of things."

Head down Nok half ran through the doorway and into the narrow soi leading to the main road. She hadn't taken more than a few steps when an arm reached out from the side, grabbed her by the waist and threw her against the wall, the man pinning her against it with his body.

"Time to pay, bitch. You promised me the money today. Let's see it."

It was Choi, the strong arm man for the money lender. Although he was never up before two in the afternoon, he had known she was in the game at Jack's; one of the players had tipped him off.

"I don't have it now. I had a bad night. Please give me one more day."

The answer was a hard slap to the face.

"Don't fuck with me. The money was due yesterday and we gave you one more day already."

He slapped her again, harder and her head bounced off the wall behind her.

"Please, I'll get it, I'll..."

Then the pressure was gone and Choi seemed to be running backwards until he hit the opposite wall of the soi. There was a man hitting him, twice in the stomach bending him over and then once in the face lifting him up against the wall. Choi gave a moan and just slid down the wall into a sitting position in a puddle of water on the pavement.

Matt stood and looked at the body of Choi slumped down in the gutter, thinking, *Man, that felt good.* Matt turned to Nok still leaning against the wall, slightly dazed.

"Nok, it's me, Matt. Are you alright?"

Matt was known to be quick with his fists. Today Nok was glad of that.

"I'm okay, Khun Matt. Thank you, but I've got to go."

Nok turned and ran towards the street before Choi could get on his feet.

Nok knew where she was going. She was going to demand an accounting from the Mor Doo before the loan shark found her.

You don't gamble with the gods or with the devil and expect to win. Nok should have known this but she was a gambler and that's what gamblers do, they gamble. Of course you always look for an inside edge, a bit of knowledge the ordinary person is not smart enough to look for or to have access to. Nok had come to see gambling as her way up in life. She knew she was smarter than the others. In essence she always felt she was betting on herself. She was special. The cards would turn up right for her. That was her belief. The belief was reinforced when she won, which was often enough to keep her coming back. And when she didn't win, when she had to beg or plead for a break or a loan to tide her over or find a customer and rent her body out to raise the necessary cash, she just knew it was the next turn of the cards or the next game that would bring her back to her true path—winning.

This time though she had been running in the red for just a bit too long and thought she had best go to a professional and check her fortune to see what her future held. What she really wanted to be told was her run of bad luck would break soon, a big payday was imminent.

She had gone to Leung Sombat, a former monk who was said to be in touch with the spirits. His readings were famous for their accuracy and his ability to cast spells—usually for good but not always—were feared by all.

The meeting with Leung Sombat had gone well for the most part. It had taken time to arrange. His was one of many small stalls adjacent to Watt Mahabut, a famous two-hundred-fifty-year-old temple in the Prakanong district of Bangkok. He didn't just sit at a stand and wait for people to come to him. Those seeking their fortune or wanting to receive a blessing had to leave a note with the woman running the stand next to his and, if he accepted the meeting, the woman would let you know when to be there. She was a Mor Doo herself but of lesser powers than Leung Sombat. His fee—five hundred baht a session—was ten times hers but she had many customers from being in the stand next to Leung Sombat's.

Nok had to wait a week for the session and almost left town twice because of the pressure from the loan shark. She had to borrow from friends twice and go out and find sex customers four times just to get the money to keep the loan shark at bay.

At the meeting, Leung Sombat, a diminutive and wrinkled

man in his sixties, had taken his time with her. First he had prayed to the Buddha shrine in the corner of his stand and she had joined in the prayer. Then he had taken her hand and looked over the palm carefully while doing so he questioned her as to her past and present. He hadn't asked if she was a gambler or a sex worker though it might be assumed he had deduced both from her age and dress though she had been careful to dress modestly for the meeting.

While normal practice, he had not collected his money up front. Although his fee was a good portion of the money she had left, she felt it was necessary to procure good fortune; it was worth it. She had to get back on the right side of the cards.

Of course he had questions. The answer to the most important one she had supplied to the woman Mor Doo who had arranged the appointment. Nok had given the Mor Doo her birth date and time of birth. This was the key information.

Birth date and time is crucial information for any advanced reading. It's information every Asian would know because it is a key indicator of one's astrological fortune. Those from the street or an uncertain background carried a great burden not having this knowledge.

"Tell me of your family."

"We are farmers from the north east, *Esan*. We are not fortunate. My father died two years ago of lung cancer. My mother is in the hospital now with cancer. I'm afraid she won't recover. My older brother is in jail for selling drugs so he could care for my mom. He's been in for two years now and has three more years to go."

Leung Sombat just nodded as if he knew all this already. He might have as it was a common, almost universal story among those young women who came to him.

He had nodded and looked into her eyes for a moment.

"Your fortune has not been good. That's why you are here."

She had just nodded, not wanting to go into further detail, afraid he might ask about her gambling.

He showed her a metal amulet crafted in the image of a

famous monk who had died some years before and was said to have achieved enlightenment. It was on a neck chain and was two inches long and two inches wide.

"This has been blessed. If you wear it, it will help your fortune, but it's expensive. Its price is ten thousand baht."

Nok just gulped. This was twice the money she had on her and she needed that money to ante up for tonight's card game.

"Can I touch it, please?"

He handed it to her. She held it reverently, rubbing it as she held it, hoping the good fortune it held would come to her immediately.

Then she laid it down on the table between them.

"I don't have that much money."

Then it happened. A scream came from the nearby row of *kutis,* the small wooden huts on stilts where the monks of the temple lived.

"Fire. Fire."

One of the temple boys was outside yelling and a few yards away one of the *kutis* was emitting smoke. A lick of flame showed itself in the doorway.

The Mor Doo stood up, moved towards the entrance of his stall and started walking towards the *kuti* on fire without looking back at Nok.

Nok looked down. The amulet lay there. In her mind it was screaming good fortune at her. She couldn't miss this chance.

She scooped up the amulet and ran out of the stall and down the small soi towards the street. She would be back and make full payment after the game tonight.

Now, in the harsh light of the following morning, she was determined she was going to expose the Mor Doo as a fraud. She had no money to pay him for their session but she would return the amulet as it had proven to be meaningless piece of metal. She was glad she hadn't bought it and was going to let the old Mor Doo and his customers know he was a fake when she found him.

As she walked up to the temple grounds, Nok could smell the scent of smoke left over from the previous afternoon's fire. The *kuti* had burned to the ground but only the one. The nearby *kutis* had escaped the flames.

To Nok's surprise, the door to the Mor Doo's stall was open. As she approached she saw him sitting inside by himself.

He was sitting quietly looking towards the door and as she walked in she had the feeling he had been waiting for her.

"Welcome back. I've been expecting you."

She tried to control her anger but couldn't help throwing the amulet down on the table in front of him.

"I shouldn't have taken it. I needed to change my fortune, but this thing turns out to be useless. You're a fraud."

He said nothing. He only tilted his head as if to better examine her. His eyes, encased in pouches of wrinkles, showed no anger. They seemed to hold a light of amusement as he stared her down.

He waved towards the chair opposite him.

"Please calm yourself. Sit down."

"I have no money left to give you, old man. That's the way it is. You promised good fortune. Well, you failed and I failed. Only I have to face the loan shark, not you."

"You've had bad fortune?"

"Yes, I've had bad fortune. I've lost everything because I believed in you and your sacred amulet. I'm finished."

"Did you lose your phone?"

"No, I have my phone. So what? Do you want that in payment?"

"Can you make a phone call for me?"

Nok was caught off guard. What game was this old man playing?

"Do you need to call somebody?"

"No. You need to call somebody."

"Who?"

"Call your mother."

Nok hesitated, but then pushed the speed dial number she had for her mom.

At the other end, her mom didn't answer, rather a man

answered the phone.

Nok was afraid. Had her mother died while she was playing cards? Was that the Mor Doo's punishment for her theft?

"Hello. Who is this? Is my mom there?"

"Nok, it's me, your brother Somchai. Don't you recognize my voice?"

"Somchai, I wasn't expecting you. What are you doing at the hospital? Has Mom died?"

"No, Nok, I'm at home with Mom. The prison granted a pardon to a large number of prisoners under a royal decree. The warden knew our mom was dying of cancer so he included me. I just got to the hospital last night."

"What is Mom doing home? I told the hospital I would pay the bills. Did they kick her out?"

"No. Mom's feeling much better. The doc said she could go home. The doc said she's in remission. When I got there they said it was okay for a family member to take her home. We're both fine but Mom wants you to come home and celebrate with us. Leave Bangkok behind for a while."

Nok was stunned. She started crying.

"Okay, Somchai. I'll call you later." She disconnected the call.

The old man watched her for a moment then reached over and picked up the amulet.

"Have you had bad news?"

"No, I... I've had good news."

Now the amused look was gone from his eyes to be replaced by a look of sadness.

"Good fortune can take many shapes. Go home, daughter. Go home today."

Big Mouth

An Austin Carr Short Mystery
Jack Getze

I hang painfully suspended by bruised and bleeding wrists, but it's the insult and mockery that *really* hurt.

"Hear that crowd?" the Professor says. "Time to get our friend."

The buzz of human vocalizing indeed sounds like post time at Seaside Park—Branchtown, New Jersey's scenic, state-owned horse track, three and a half miles off the Garden State Parkway. I could be down by the grandstand rail, clutching my winning ticket, rooting some maiden claimer home in today's final race. But no, I'm hanging from the rear wall of this abandoned horse barn, a spread-eagle captive of the Professor.

"Someone to see you," the Professor says.

Some*thing*, more accurately. The Professor walks a well-groomed thoroughbred into the stall I decorate like a tapestry, the smile on the Professor's face an affront in itself. The filly—a light red chestnut, or sorrel—snorts and shakes her head, her lips foaming as if she's already been antagonized. Like every redhead I ever met.

The Professor spins the filly around so I'm facing her rear end, my captor no doubt preparing to add grave physical injury to the psychological jibe of my impending death, the irony of which still staggers me. I mean, this horse better hurry if she wants to kill me because the sarcasm of this filly's triple-punch moniker already has pierced my heart: I can't *believe* Jersey's most famous investment counselor—me, a man known for his gift of gab, his uncanny ability to escape the most dire circumstances with words and grins—is about to be kicked to death by a horse named Zip Your Lip.

I try to calm myself with deep breathing, but the odor of stale urine stings my sinuses. I believe the stench comes from the old stained straw below me, but I can't be sure. I've been stuck up on this horse-house wall a long time, exhibiting seriously nervous behavior since I realized the Professor had taken charge of my future. I'm saying I could have peed my pants.

"You'll last longer if you resist screaming," the Professor says. "Screaming upsets her."

"I'll try to hold it down."

"Ha ha ha."

The Professor's moist cackle gives me the willies. Who knew how creepy human beings could become? As a central Jersey stockbroker, I thought I'd seen and heard every kind of ugly cheat the world offered: Stolen kidneys auctioned to finance private annuities, phony stock certificates, forged wills and last testaments, condom interiors coated with hot sauce. But nothing compares to this execution, I think. The Professor is special, a doctor of strange deaths.

"When does the show start?" I ask.

"Oh, you'll know right away. When I give Zip Your Lip the electric shock, the first thing she does is kick. I believe it's a muscle reflex."

I love the scientific details. It's why I call the Professor the Professor.

And I thought my future looked shitty at the lunch party today.

Three Hours Earlier

My friend and restaurateur Luis Guerrero is one hard hombre, a warrior. His ancient-American cheek bones and black eyes don't often broadcast expression, let alone emotion, so when he publicly scowls at his brother-in-law Heriberto, anger radiating from Luis like heat from a flag-burning crowd, I swallow a double shot of worry—not only for Heriberto, who might die right here in Luis' restaurant, but also for tonight's special luncheon, *carnitas y quacamole*. My favorite. I've barely tasted the exquisite holiday feast Luis' chef has prepared.

"You have spent all of the money I sent to Rosalinda?" Luis says.

My friend's dark eyes shine at his brother-in-law Heriberto like polished river stones. Tendons flex on both sides of Luis' neck. This could bust up our lunch party *muy pronto.* Our crew is already starting to fidget: There's my friend Luis, his wife Solana; Luis' sister Rosalinda; Rosalinda's second husband Heriberto Garzia, the man on the spot; plus me— Austin Carr. I don't think of tonight's twelve-pound pork roast as my date yet, but it could come to that.

"It was most expensive to travel to the United States," Heriberto says. "Especially from Texas to New Jersey. It has been difficult to find a job. There was rent and food."

Our party occupies a round table smack in the middle of my pal Luis's popular restaurant, Luis' Mexican Grill, and though the two men try to keep their voices down, half a dozen heads lift from plates of enchiladas or tacos to gaze our way. It's not unusual for women to have their eye on Luis. He's always tall, dark, and handsome. But today being the fifth of May, and a Friday, the restaurant bulges with Cinco de Mayo revelers.

Luis sneers at his brother-in-law. "Over thirty thousand American dollars for food and rent? You insult me. You insult all of us with these exaggerations. Did you gamble the money away—again?"

Heriberto wrinkles his forehead. The short hair on his neck bristles. "Before we came here, I used much of that money to pay for the annual school tuition for your nieces."

Luis wears his restaurant uniform—black slacks with a black vest over a white dress shirt. Out of habit, the shirt's long sleeves are rolled up, showing off his Popeye, forearm muscles that discourage would-be rowdies. Luis in charge is like being eight years old and having your fifteen-year-old brother on the playground with you. If you do have trouble with peers, they won't be a problem long.

"Only one year of tuition?" Luis says. "What about the remaining two payments? How will the rest of their education be paid for? And yet your clothes are expensive. So is the watch on your wrist. Were these things purchased with the money I sent Rosalinda as well?"

I take another mouthful of delicious, slow roasted pork. This feast approaches meltdown. In ten years, I have never seen Luis so upset. Well, maybe once or twice.

Heriberto glares at Luis across our party's dish and glass cluttered table. "I bought this one suit and a timepiece so I might search for a good job."

Luis stands, a vein pulsing in his forehead. I wonder why Luis' sister Rosalinda doesn't speak up for her husband. She stares trancelike into her uneaten pork. "You do not need a suit or a watch to work at the race track stables," Luis says. "I know where you have been spending your time—where you *always* spend your time—as well spend others' money. But the horses do not care how you dress, Heriberto—or what time it is. The money which I saved and sent to my sister was for the education of my nieces, who are your daughters now, it seems I must remind you. I question why you do not act and speak of them as a father would."

Heriberto shoves back his chair and stands, matching Luis, facing him like a gunfighter. Heriberto clenches his hands. "I am Rosalinda's husband—yes, and Yolanda and Esmeralda's legal father. I will say and do what I choose with my family's money. As for my daughters' education, the girls will join us here next year and attend American schools without charge. My efforts at employment have been successful."

"What employment?" Luis says. "To dress like an American executive and clean horse stalls?"

Heriberto's chest puffs. "You know very *well* I am a graduate of Mexico's largest university, a former chemist and animal dietician for Sagarpa—the Secretaria de Agricultura Gana—"

"*Si, si.*" Luis cuts him off. "And you would have graduated a year earlier had you not gambled away the money I loaned you."

"As of next week," Heriberto says, "I will be Assistant Science Officer for one of the largest thoroughbred stables in New Jersey."

Luis' gaze narrows. The three tables nearest ours have

broken off eating and talking among themselves to watch us. I self-consciously stop chewing my pork. Dietician I understand, but what exactly does a science officer do to horses? Breed them?

"And it is ill-mannered to belittle a member of your *family* before our wives and your friend," Heriberto says.

For the first time this evening, Heriberto's wife Rosalinda—Luis' sister—lifts her gaze toward her husband. Her eyes are black darts, peering out from under half-shut lids. Her lips quiver as she says, "Tell us all, Heriberto. Does *your family* include the whore you slept with last night?"

Normally, Branchtown residents like myself enjoy watching conflict. If a fight's coming, we like to gather. But this family tiff will remove my *favorite* Mexican dish, food for the gods, my first choice at all of life's many banquets. I force another chunk of crispy pork into an already crowded mouth.

Rosalinda points a finger at her husband. "You say *nothing?*"

The volume of her voice silences any chatter remaining in Luis' popular restaurant. Save for a few guys watching last night's Yankees rerun at the bar, lost in their beer and baseball, *everybody* is now staring at us, our table a stage.

"Is this true?" Luis says. His voice shakes the half-filled water glass in front of me. Ripples vibrate on the surface. "You committed adultery within a year of your vows to my sister—vows before God and our priest?"

The room—our audience—produces an audible gasp, like gusting wind through the window. Rosalinda snatches her dinner knife, lifts the blade above her shoulder to throw.

Luis grabs his sister around the shoulders and holds her close. She struggles in his arms. Rosalinda's knuckles squeeze themselves white against the knife handle, the blade inches from her brother's cheek. Rosalinda's Native American facial features pinch together in torture—a knot of thick brown rope.

"Get him out of here." Luis is shouting. "The man is a pig."

I have never heard Luis scream in anger. My senses are dulled by shock and adrenaline, not to mention a yearning for more crispy pork and the earlier consumption of four or five tequilas. That I can't remember exactly how many cactus cocktails tells me the number might be seven or eight. My addled brain needs several seconds to understand the Heriberto-removal order was meant for me.

I stand and call a cab on my cell phone. *No way* I'm driving.

Luis hisses on our way outside. *"Puerco."*

Our Branchtown cabbie smells like he's popped a few bourbons himself tonight, maybe spilled the bottle on his pants. Plus he's eighty-five years old. I'm not so sure Heriberto and I are better off with him driving: My younger reflexes, though alcohol-impaired, could be functionally superior.

Nah.

"I need to be at Seaside Park within the hour," Heriberto says. "I am meeting a trainer named Oscar Ruiz right after the feature race."

"*The* Oscar Ruiz? Of Atlantis Farms?"

"*Si.* Yes."

"That's some first job in America," I say. "Congratulations." Ruiz is well known, even among casual horse racing fans like myself. Extremely successful in reaching the winner's circle the past year, Ruiz is now considered one of the top horse trainers on the east coast.

"I am an educated man, Senor Carr. Not all immigrants from Mexico are day laborers. Perhaps you would like to come with me and meet Oscar? He could have need of investment advice."

I consider my companion. Heriberto's black hair is cut level on top like a 1950s teenager, including the gooey, brushed up front edge—a flat top, my father called the hairstyle. Below Heriberto's mustache, which is neat and trim, like one stroke of a felt-tip pen, Luis's brother-in-law curiously sports a wide, infectious smile. I wonder how much tequila Heriberto has consumed.

"What are you so happy about?" I ask.

"Rosalinda. She loves me very much."

The old cabbie snorts. I lean close to see if Heriberto foams at the mouth. "You're kidding me, right? She could have killed you with that knife."

"Because she is jealous. Austin Carr does not understand women, I see. So much anger is clear evidence that she is deeply in love."

Did I miss something? To me, love is more like kissing and hugging, doing the horizontal boogie. Or, when you get older, maybe taking your kids to the beach.

"Have you ever made love to a true redhead?" Heriberto asks. "Ever kissed the soft, pure whiteness at the very base of her thigh?"

My mother, a southern belle from Mississippi, taught me some things are better left unheard. This Heriberto is definitely over the top, a real Romeo.

"Last night was perhaps my most beautiful of redheaded lovers, the softest of white thighs ever," he says.

I feel sorry for Rosalinda, whose hair is definitely not red. Heriberto is right about those redheaded thighs, though. Our cabby prepares to wheel us into a main Seaside Park gate, but Heriberto re-directs him to the backside, or stables.

"I ask you as a family friend," Heriberto says. "Come with me to meet Oscar. I know this famous trainer from long ago, when we were children in Mexico, and he has agreed to hire me. But it will impress him that I know a man of your importance here in America."

"Importance? I'm just a stockbroker."

"*Por favor,*" he says. "Tonight is *very* special."

Oh why not? Luis will save some carnitas for me.

Heriberto and I split the ten-dollar cab ride, walk between two dozen expensive parked cars to a guard-hut the size of a pickup truck. A gray-haired, chunky, uniformed security cop discovers Heriberto's name on a list, passes us into the primary stable area. Most people never see the backside. It's bigger than the rest of the racetrack combined, an entire city in itself, populated during racing season by people and horses twenty-four hours a day, seven days a week. The backside covers twice the land, never sleeps and has its own fire department as big as any nearby towns.

Heriberto and I march down the main street, a broken-asphalt and dirt road, fifty yards beyond the track's backstretch, but much lower, hidden from the distant grandstands and clubhouse. Double-rows of white-painted barns—and the lawn areas between—occupy every inch of space on our right, each barrack-style building consisting of forty or so separate compartments. Green awnings block the sun from the horse stalls, not to mention the muckers, hot-walkers, and hangers-on, although most have retired for the day by mid-afternoon.

A six-foot-high chain link fence parallels the road as we pass the last working barn. Beyond a burned out tack shack the size of a tree house, we reach another row of white-washed, asphalt-tile-roof horse stalls. But the paint here is peeling, the roof patched with uneven chunks of used plywood. There are no horses in the stalls, no work being done on the roof or the blackened tack room.

"Maybe I read too many mystery novels," I say. "But why would Oscar Ruiz want to meet you way out here. The Atlantis Farms section wasn't far from where we came in."

"He wants no one to know of our meeting."

"That's kind of weird, isn't it? Did you ask why?"

Heriberto shakes his flat-topped head. "I think it is possible Oscar does not want all of his owners to know about me yet."

"Wait. Which owner or owners is Oscar Ruiz worried about?"

"A man who is called the Turk."

In my overly-dramatic, exaggerated manner, I halt all forward movement.

"Why do you stop—like a clown?" Heriberto says.

I stare at Luis' brother-in-law. I'd rather act like a clown than take another secret step in the direction of Johnny "The Turk" Korsay—or anything he's a part of. The Turk *was* the local crime boss's accountant and chief bookmaker, a street wise Lebanese with a genius for odds, costs, and horses. I say *was* because when his boss Bluefish died last year, the Turk—another non-Italian—won the local boss's job on a temporary basis. But he earns New York so much money, his Italian chiefs haven't bothered replacing him. I know this stuff through my personal and slightly unreliable connection to organized crime—Angelina "Mama Bones" Bonacelli, local bingo-game fixer and the mother of my business partner, Vic.

"You know this Turk?" Heriberto asks.

"Yes, and sneaking behind the Turk's back could get you killed, *amigo*. I am *not* going to your meeting."

"This Turk is... what, a *pistolero*?"

"Worse. He owns an *army* of gunmen."

Ahead of us, a smallish man strides from the shadows of the abandoned racing barn. My heart rate bumps up. "Perhaps two armies," the new man says.

"Aye." Heriberto reaches out for him. Must be Oscar, the trainer, as the two obvious friends hold their embrace and pat each other's back. Heriberto is half a head taller and fifty pounds heavier than his boyhood pal. There is more backslapping before they separate.

"Oscar, I would like to introduce to you Austin Carr, a friend," Heriberto says. "He manages many millions of dollars for the important people of Branchtown."

A commuter train hisses by us on the nearby NJ Transit line. Crows squawk, disturbed from the trees by the rush of sound and wind. Offering me his hand to shake, Oscar smiles and nods, but his eyes work the dark around us.

"Oscar, it was a pleasure to meet you," I say, "but I need to get the get the hell out of here."

Spinning to avoid astonished expressions or any further delay, my exit is blocked. A hulking shadow splits off from the dark by the burned tack room to meet me at the edge of the circle of yellow light, this man-shape six and a half feet tall, maybe three hundred pounds. His weight and enormous arms jostle me back into the brightness with Heriberto and Oscar. He dresses like an insurance salesman—gray slacks and a three-button blazer—except his fists are the size of lamps.

"Stay," he says. "The Turk wants an introduction."

At the second mention of Branchtown's prince of organized crime—Mama Bones tells me all the *kings* live in

New York—I am out of wise cracks. The man with big hands—Lamp Fists—shuffles into my breathing space. His sandpaper chin rubs my nose.

"Raise your arms," he says. "I'm gonna search you."

His breath flows over my scalp like a low-set hairdryer. His fingers rake my trunk, legs and crotch like gardening claws.

Another six-foot-plus man joins us, thinner and wrapped tight like cable wire, this second guy wearing jeans and a black leather jacket, fuzzy red dreadlocks for hair, and holding a pistol. The two thugs—Lamp Fists and the thinner Red Dreads—hustle me and Heriberto underneath the last barn's green canopy, then down a line of abandoned stalls. Mexican mariachi music floats in the air, a distant thumping of the bass, the horns on top, but there's no one back here to see us walking.

We reach a twelve-foot-square building breaking up two long sections of horse barracks, the little house also painted green and white. Oscar leads us inside, flips on a dim overhead light after all five of us enter and the door is secured. Bright racing silks and worn riding crops are tacked to one wall. Posed by an oak roll top desk, like a model in *Gentleman's Quarterly*, stands a man I assume to be the Turk. He smokes a cigarette.

Pointing at me with a wrinkled forehead, Turk says, "Who's *this* guy?"

Though I've never met him, this impeccably adorned individual *has* to be the Turk: Six-foot-four, an athletic two hundred and fifty pounds, wearing a light gray, cashmere and silk suit that fits him like clothes made and tailored on Savile Row, London, England—which they were if this is the Turk. I hear he spends ten to twenty thousand dollars per suit of clothes. Depends on the cloth.

Hard steel pokes my back. "Tell the Turk your name."

I turn to Lamp Fists. "I thought you said he wanted—"

A kidney punch from Red Dreads refocuses my attention. I gasp to regain my breath. "I'm Austin Carr."

The Turk's black eyes glare into mine as he slips a hand into the suit from Savile Row. The Jersey Shore air breathes sticky this late afternoon, but humid weather probably doesn't explain the chasers of sweat rolling down my flanks. I remind myself to breathe as Turk's hand reappears with a thin, black tube. I can't tell if the thing's a ballpoint pen or—

He shines the thin flashlight in my eyes. "You're Austin Carr? Mama Bones' bond shop partner?"

"Actually, Mama Bones' son Vic is my partner, although sometimes it feels like Mama Bones does whatever the hell she wants around there. She even—"

"Shut up," Turk says. "What are you doing here with Oscar and the Mexican juicer?"

Juicer? So Heriberto is that kind of chemist—one who makes the horses go faster, longer, or both through injected chemical science. Obviously, this is one of those rare occasions when truth actually *is* the best policy. I'll be fine. All I have to do is not talk too much. "Heriberto asked me to come with him, as a favor. He didn't tell me Oscar was *your* trainer, or that he was—is—what you say, you know, a juicer. I never would have come if I had known that. Hell, I was turning around to leave when—"

"Shut *up*," Turk says. "Jeez, you gotta big mouth. You know who I *am*?"

"Sure. You're the Turk, Johnny Korsay, the guy who took over local crime operations after Bluefish got shot in the head, the guy who once punched a horse to death when it finished—"

He waves a hand in front of my face. "I can't believe your mouth. You must be fucking mental."

"My mom always said it's part of my charm."

I swear I have no idea where these self-destructive outbursts come from. It's like my mouth is an independent, potentially suicidal organ answering to no other region—particularly not my brain. The Turk's rugged face twists sideways. He blinks, then his mouth buckles into a sneer. I can see Turk wonders, as any mob boss would, where do I get the balls to insult him by continuing to talk, especially about my own charm and my mother.

"Your mom?" The Turk shakes his head. "Jesus, big mouth doesn't cover your problem, does it?"

Hey, I wonder where this crazy streak comes from, too. As myself, my friends, and even total strangers have witnessed many times, my mind and mouth ramble all by themselves. Especially when I'm nervous. The Gift of Gab—of Blab— exists completely on its own, ruled by impulse. Which means that, like a puppy, it can go poo-poo any time, even in my own house.

The Turk sticks out his palm to Red Dreads. "Gimme your gun."

Uh, oh.

Turk clutches the offered semiautomatic pistol. He lifts the weapon, shoots Heriberto in the temple, then smacks Oscar in the forehead with it. Both men fall to the bare wood floor, Luis' brother-in-law half a second faster and without bones— like a rag.

Jesus! My gut drops to the floor. I twist and try to run, but Lamp Fist grabs me firmly by the neck. The room's air fogs with exploded gunpowder, more smell than smoke. I can't breathe. Turk moves the gun closer, the muzzle chilling the oily covering of my forehead. This is it, big mouth. No talking yourself out of this one.

"Wait a minute," Turk whispers. He shifts the semiautomatic's aim higher, over my head.

I suck air like a new vacuum cleaner. The air tastes bitter, a sulfur flavor that roils my stomach. Or maybe it's the blood and gray brains on the floor beside me. My God, Heriberto murdered—the flat-topped Romeo I rode in a cab with fifteen minutes ago.

"What's the matter?" Red Dreads says to Turk. "Worried about the disposal arrangements? I got cement and garbage bags in my trunk."

The Turk shakes his head, lets the weapon fall to his thigh. "I'm in a sick fucking mood, that's what. I can't believe that table-topped Mexican had the balls to bribe my trainer, cheat me on his new epitestosterone-based masker, then last night take my girlfriend home from the track party."

"The Mexican must be crazy," Red Dreads says.

The Turk's gaze wanders back to me. "And then *this* asshole can't keep his yap shut, says he's a local, knows who I am, but acts like Johnny Korsay is nobody. Wants to tell me about his mother."

Red Dreads winks at his friend Lamp Fists.

"It pisses me off," Turk says. "This prick thinks him being friends with Mama Bones is going to protect him. Well I got news for you and Mama Bones, asshole."

He grabs my face. "Jim Mallory was a friend of mine."

Nobody has seen Mallory in a few months. Guess the Turk thinks Mama Bones had something to do with his disappearance.

"I need to work out my anger," Turk says, "maybe kick this bastard to death."

That sounds unpleasant. I figured a bullet to the skull would at least kill me fast.

"No—wait," Turk says. "I'm gonna have a horse do it."

Good thing my bladder was already empty.

The Turk whacks my temple with the barrel of his pistol. Pain explodes as a red blotch behind my eyes, the color turning purple, then black as I sink again to one knee.

"I know exactly the right thoroughbred, too," the Turk says. "A fitting end for this asshole's big mouth."

I curl up asleep on the smelly dirt.

The Turk is still there when I wake up, his distinctively gruff voice droning close by. I can't touch myself. I can't walk, crawl, scratch, pinch or even paw the air. My hands are tied to something well above my head, arms outstretched against a hard surface, my body extended vertically. My feet dangle midair, heels together, both bumping against the same wall as my hands. Uh, oh. My eyes blink open to confirm: I am tied spread-eagle against the back of a straw-floored horse stall. Looks like the Turk wasn't kidding about having a thoroughbred kick me to death.

Jeez, did this day turn ugly. My guts are sick inside thinking of Heriberto. The split-second look of terror on his face. I tug with force on whatever binds my wrists, but cry out in pain and halt my effort. I'm bound by thin metal wire, solidly attached to four-inch hooks screwed into the wood. A trickle of blood slides along my right arm, down from wrist to armpit and inside my Tommy Bahama shirt, a palm tree and hula-girl affair I purchased especially for Luis' Cinco de Mayo party. The pain—and the shirt—would be a small price to pay for the chance of freedom, but nothing budged when I yanked.

I can't have much time either.

The Turk leans into the stall where I'm on exhibit, his elbows on the bottom half of the old horse-barn's Dutch door. "Hear that crowd?" he says. "Time to get our friend, Zip Your Lip. The noise should cover your screams."

The Turk—who needs a new nickname—leads a horse into my stall, a light red chestnut. He spins the filly around so I'm facing her rear end, the horse's head pointed toward the stall door. Talk about humiliation: I can't *believe* Jersey's most famous investment counselor—me—is about to be killed by a horse named Zip Your Lip. The irony hurts my teeth.

"If this trap tonight was for Heriberto," I ask, "how come I'm the one stuck up here like living art?"

He laughs. "Wrong place, wrong time, Carr. I can't wipe out what you saw. You were most likely a dead man the moment you came along with that juicer. Although it is your big fucking *mouth* which is going to cost you monumental pain."

Maybe I can stall him. "Heriberto designed his own epitestosterone-based masker? I thought those chemicals could be detected in the blood tests after a race?"

"You know about juice?" Turk asks.

"A little."

"You're a horse guy, huh?"

"Enough to know Oscar had a whole lot of winners in Florida," I say, "and he seems to have brought his winning streak to Jersey."

The Turk laughs. I'm thinking I might have stumbled onto a mineable vein when his smile disappears like a magician's rabbit. "You're a lying piece of crap, Carr. You think Mama Bones is going to protect you? Too bad. Jim Mallory deserves some payback. And hell, you're probably here because you and Mama Bones want to cut yourself into Heriberto's skimming me."

What? "No way. I came because Heriberto asked me, because he's a relative of my friend, because I like the horses. I didn't—"

He turns his neatly tailored back on me. "Die screaming you little turd."

The Turk disappears from our stall doorway—*our* meaning me and my roomy, Zip Your Lip—but I soon hear Turk giving instructions to his men about taking me and Heriberto's remains to Sandy Hook for burial—eavesdropping that immediately has me trying to rip off my right arm. While I wouldn't call the constraint loose, ten seconds of wiggling, bleeding, and stifling my own screams slightly shifts the screwed-into-the-wood hook. The barn is old, the wood aged and beginning to rot.

I yank with all my strength, crying out from the pain, but the variation I created earlier is gone. Nothing. I've jiggled the hook into a permanent lock-up.

"Hang on, Austin," Turk says. Of course he heard me holler. "I'll be right there."

My body relaxes, a limp carcass on the back wall of life. I know when the game is over. I've been in a couple of these life-or-death situations. Once a friend saved me. In an episode or two, I *talked* my way out. But this time, I believe I'm roasted. Luis told me to get Heriberto out of there, so my friend and potential hero Luis Guerrero will be protecting his sister, not worrying about me. It's important to be optimistic in life, but right now, I am in so much pain, I almost wish the Turk would shoot me.

Turk slides into view, in his hand a rock-size hunk of silver. Must be the electric shocker he talked about. He stretches his well-tailored arm inside the stall, reaching for Zip Your Lip's neck. The filly shies from his hand, compressing my ribcage with her weight, shutting off my airways. So much for giving up. I struggle unsuccessfully against the horse's butt and the wire restraints with every cell of my being.

The Turk stretches farther inside the stall, extending himself through the half-open door. I'm rooting for contact, as the horse currently crushes me, and I get my wish—Turk's buzzer slaps Zip Your Lip where shoulder meets neck. In the midst of a life-or-death effort to breathe, my addled, frightened brain clearly hears the sound, a soft metallic *zzzzz*.

Zip Your Lip's weight pushes harder against my chest, testing my ribs, blackening the edges of my vision —but then lunges forward. Her massive chest crashes the stall gate. I suck in a delicious gulp of air, but success is fleeting. The filly's ears cock low and back. Her shoulders dip, shifting her weight to the front legs. A kick cometh.

I tug on the once-loose wall hook one more time, as hard as I am able. I don't expect to have much energy left, but the potential of death seems a powerful motivator. I grant this last yank everything my heart possesses, and I scream out loud from the pain, the wire digging half an inch into my bleeding flesh.

Zip Your Lip tucks her rump.

I'm still heaving the wire as hard as I can, still screaming...

The right hook snaps free of the wood. Loose, my weight falls to the left, pivoting on the hook still attached to the wall. The filly's two back feet clobber the old stall, one hoof breaking wood inches from my swinging shoulder. My shoes hit the ground. I'm attached to the stall by the remaining hook—but my feet carry weight now. The searing pain eases, and I'm able to dance out of her way when Zip Your Lip kicks again.

She keeps kicking. The Turk curses, his voice clear above the continuing sound of fragmenting boards. He unlatches the Dutch door's bottom—coming inside now, reaching for something in his chest pocket. That gun?

My free hand wears a bracelet of bloody wire and a loose screw, and though burdened, my fingers work hard to free my other arm from the wall. Then I have a better idea: When I stab the filly's butt with the sharp screw, Zip Your Lip cries high-pitched like the wounded three-year-old she is.

Sorry, horsey.

The filly rears, kicking Turk with a front hoof on the way up. He falls limp, the weapon he borrowed from Red Dreads tumbling from his grip. Zip Your Lip charges, stomping the

Turk and crashing through a poorly timed inspection outside the stall from Lamp Fists. The big man manages a grunt of surprise before getting horse-bumped to the ground.

I free myself. Numb but pumped with adrenaline, I stagger to the semi-conscious Turk, pick up his spilled weapon, then peek outside. There's no sign of Red Dreads, only Lamp Fists in the dirt, groaning, holding a leg that looks broken. The world spins a little crazy. I'm confused, or in shock.

Clomping hooves catch my ear. Zip Your Lip gallops around the next white barn thirty yards over and disappears from my sight.

"What the hell..." a voice says behind me.

It's Red Dreads, hurrying around the barn opposite, double-timing his jog back to his comrades. The tall wiry man stops and begins to screw a noise-suppressor onto the muzzle of another semiautomatic pistol. He doesn't see Luis step from the darkness behind him. The crack of Luis' muckers shovel knocks Red Dread to the ground. The man in black leather melts like pudding.

Luis picks up Red's weapon, gazes at me. "How badly are you injured?"

"I need a doctor for these wrists, but I'm okay. But Heriberto is dead. The Turk shot him. We need to call the police."

"I have already done so."

"How did you know I was in trouble?" I ask.

"You did not return for a second helping of *carnitas y quacamole.*"

I want to laugh but I can't. Could be a while before I enjoy humor that way again. Watching Heriberto die changed my life, I know it.

"Hey, Carr!"

It's the Turk, on his elbows and knees, injured. He's crawled outside the stall behind me. That twenty-thousand-dollar Savile Row suit will need a two-hundred-dollar cleaning, maybe a furnace. "You're a lucky bastard, you know that?" His raspy voice scratches at the air. "Get me out of here before the cops come, I won't have you killed."

Luis strides past me to stand above the local crime figure.

Slowly, my friend lowers Red Dreads' noise-suppressed semiautomatic to aim at the center of Turk's chest. "I see one dead man on each side," Luis says. "My friend is injured and so are you. Would not your interests be best served by agreeing to a permanent truce? Let me add that my decision will be based upon yours."

I'm not sure the Turk understands Luis' words. My pal puts his English together in odd constructions. But clearly Turk grasps the message of that semiautomatic hovering in his eyes.

"All right," the Turk says. "This is over."

Our Lady of Blessed Opportunity
Frank De Blase

The Virgin Mary gazed down sadly at the whole affair. Out of the corner of his eye, Charlie Ferelli thought he saw the twinkle of a tear in the corner of Her eye. He shook his head until it was gone. This was the Mother of God after all; She had seen sadder things—Biblically more tragic—than this two-bit hoodlum's send-off at C. Ferelli & Sons Funeral Home in Brooklyn. Why would She shed tears for him? Besides, She was only a painting; a big oil painting in an ornate gold frame the deceased had requested in his will be hung over the casket amidst the avalanche of flowers and wreaths with their note cards of heartfelt sympathy. Beloved this, beloved that. Bon voyage.

The turf war which had punctuated the thick August air with gunfire and spattered the sidewalks with blood almost every night for a month had finally settled down. Retributions had been made, scores settled, territory divvied up, the fat trimmed and the herd thinned out. Cease fire. It would be awhile before things heated up again. But in the meantime, here lay Anthony "Manny" Mangione: hustler, mob soldier, stiff.

It wasn't all that clear—the mob doesn't employ a press agent—but this particular hit seemed to be a disciplinary action, an example made for a slip in loyalty or a simple fuck-up. Since most mob hits wound up at Ferelli's it was safe to assume this was mob business and nobody else's.

Charlie stayed on to run C. Ferelli & Sons on his own after his old man croaked—ironically at work—and his brother couldn't get past the heebie-jeebies he got around dead bodies. Dead bodies like Manny Mangione.

The line to view the star attraction in his mahogany coffin

wrapped down the hall to the crowded vestibule. The crowd, a mixture of family and "business" associates, was dressed entirely in black. The conversation was sharp and loud; a cocktail party with one less drunk. However, the scene became increasingly somber the closer you got to the open casket.

As was the custom, professional mourners were hired and placed about the room to let out sobs and forlorn wails of anguish when the mother of the deceased, his wife and a couple of girlfriends, who had all just met, needed a break from putting on the waterworks.

His hands clasped behind him, Charlie milled about, making sure things remained copasetic; not everyone was friends here. He headed for the front door; the cops were there. Charlie knew in a situation like this, the button man would frequently show up boldly and pay respects to the very individual he had ventilated two days before. Just as his presence might be known, detectives let theirs be known as well. O'Hanlon, the big pasty one in charge, buttonholed Charlie.

"What do you know about this, Charlie?" he asked with a cigarette that was more ash than cigarette bobbing from the corner of his mouth.

"Nothin'," Charlie shot back. "I just make 'em pretty. They usually don't talk to me once they get here. If they did, I'm afraid it'd be splitsville for me."

One of the other detectives chuckled before O'Hanlon glared him into silence. O'Hanlon started to smooth Charlie's tie before yanking its skinny end, jamming the knot tight to his windpipe.

"Don't fuck with me, Ferelli," he said. "Or you'll be looking for someone to make you pretty."

Charlie squirmed.

"I told ya," he said hoarsely. "I don't know nothin'."

"Well," O'Hanlon said. "I want you to keep your ear to the ground. It seems close to a quarter of a million dollars went missing during a routine numbers racket transfer last week. It was determined to be an inside job with Mangione at the wrong end of the finger-pointing and ultimately the wrong end of a gun. And from what I hear, the hard boys are hot."

O'Hanlon scratched his chin as if something had just occurred to him.

"Perhaps, Charlie," he said. "You're going to be getting more business."

Charlie was confused.

"What do you mean?" he asked.

"That two fifty large is still at large. And they're not just going to let this slide, no sir."

The fuzz flew and Charlie went back to the business of funeral directing. As he made his way over to the casket, he glanced up at the Virgin Mary. She looked back at him, concerned.

Viewing hours were scheduled until 9 p.m. that evening. They would briefly resume at 9 a.m. the next morning before the procession to the church for mass, then on to a plot in the skull orchard.

Charlie looked around at the different faces without staring directly. Could the killer actually be here? It was getting hot and emotions were getting ramped up.

One of the pro mourners let out a wail. The others joined in, invoking the name of God and Manny, poor Manny. After successfully ignoring each other for most of the evening, Mangione's two girlfriends opted for a punch-up and hair-pulling session with his widow before some of the mourners intervened. It was a trio of trouble that would trifle the dead man no more. The Virgin Mary just rolled her eyes.

The next morning, Charlie, his assistant Freddy, the parish priest, and six pallbearers all built like gorillas, gathered around the casket along with Mangione's wife and mother and a few random relatives.

As he had been instructed in Mangione's will, Charlie took down the painting of the Virgin Mary and laid it in the casket, across the dead man's chest. The women cried as the priest mumbled his papist voodoo and slung holy water. Charlie and

Freddy looked up at each other; shit, the picture was too wide... *shit.* They couldn't close the casket. Everyone looked around the room. Mangione's wife was sobbing.

"He loved that painting," she said.

A light bulb went on in Charlie's head.

"Look," he said. "The frame is too big, but the painting isn't. We can take the painting out of the frame, roll it up and it'll fit perfect." Everyone looked around. There were no objections... or other suggestions.

Charlie took the painting and headed for the stairs leading to his workshop.

"I'll be right back," he said.

Charlie studied the painting on the workbench. The back was fastened on by too many little brackets to pull out, so he laid it flat under a towel and got a hammer to crack the frame. He tapped it gently, nothing. He tapped it a little harder and the glass cracked a bit. The Virgin Mary winked. Charlie whacked it a third time even harder and the frame let out a dull crack and broke in two. The painting slid out easily, along with bundled stacks and stacks of fifty dollar bills, onto the floor; the missing mob money and Mangione's admission to the afterlife.

Charlie thought quick on his feet. He scooped up the money and threw it in an empty casket, rolled the canvas up and headed back upstairs to Mangione and his mourners. He slid the rolled up painting under the dead man's arm and he and Freddy closed the lid and sealed it. Over the family's sobs and the priest's dark incantations, Charlie swore he could hear the Virgin Mary laughing.

San Quentin Blues
Bill Moody

One

Dan Cooper awakened suddenly, unsure for a moment where he was. He blinked, trying to remember how long he'd been asleep. He turned his head and looked at the clock radio glowing on the night stand. Eleven twenty. He sighed. Less than an hour. He knew there wouldn't be more, at least not now. He turned the other way and looked at the woman lying beside him, trying to remember her name.

She was on her side, facing away from him, her long dark hair half over her eyes, her breathing deep in a sound sleep. A few hours ago, they had shared several beers, a Mexican meal, and later, her bed. But now, he couldn't remember her name. Carol? Cathy? Connie? No, never Connie? Cathy. Yes that was it. Cooper watched her for a minute, then sat up slowly and quietly and slipped out of bed.

He searched the darkened bedroom for his jeans and shirt, then sat down in a chair near the bed and pulled on his socks and loafers. He found his jacket on the back of the chair, checked for his gun and badge and stood up, just as her eyes opened.

She glanced at him, then at the clock. "You leaving already? It's early."

"I know. Didn't want to spoil your sleep."

She raised up, leaning on her elbow, facing him, letting the sheet slip down, almost exposing her breasts.

"Gotta go," he said. He leaned down and kissed her lightly on the forehead.

"Will I see you again?"

He straightened up and looked at her. "Probably not."

She laid her head back down on the pillow and gazed at him. "Will you call me sometime?"

"Sure."

"No you won't."

Cooper didn't answer. He turned and headed for the door.

"Hey."

He stopped and turned back.

"You have great hands."

Twenty minutes later Cooper let himself into his small condo and opened the sliding door that offered a view of Marina del Rey, just south of Santa Monica. He stepped out onto the tiny balcony, leaned on the railing, and took a deep breath. There was a definite chill in the night air. He gazed for a few moments at the scores of craft moored in the marina. Everything from tiny sail boats to ocean going luxury yachts. As always, Cooper felt the familiar twinge of longing before he went back inside and slid the door shut.

He grabbed a bottle of beer from the fridge, opened it, and walked over to the worn leather couch and sat down, leaning his head back, and stared at the television opposite him. He picked up the remote, pressed the power button, and began flicking through the channels, trying to find something he hadn't already seen, or wanted to see. He finally gave up and settled for ESPN, a show analyzing last week's NFL games.

He dropped the remote on the coffee table next to his cell phone, kicked off his shoes, and leaned back again, closing his eyes, almost giving in to the dozy feeling washing over him. He knew he should fight it or he'd end up with a sore neck and a couple of hours of fitful sleep. Nothing like a night off.

He'd just about dozed off when the phone rang. He sat up quickly and fumbled for his phone. "This is Cooper."

"It's Officer Tucker. Sorry to bother you at home so late, Lieutenant."

"Then why did you?"

"A woman called asking for you, wanted your number. I told her I'd give you her number. I hope that was okay."

"She asked for me by name? What did she want?"

"Wouldn't say. Just said she needed to talk to you. Said it was urgent."

"She leave a name?"

Cooper heard a shuffling of papers. "Bishop. Connie Bishop."

Suddenly, Cooper was very awake. "Number?" He got up and walked over to a small desk to search for a pen and pad, then copied down the number. "All right, Tucker, thanks. I'll take it from here."

Connie Bishop. He sat down again and thought about her. How many years had it been? Not since high school, and that was too long ago to think about. At Santa Monica High School, Connie Bishop had been a flag twirler, and part of the homecoming queen's court. Tall, blonde, long legs, Cooper had fallen under her spell the first time he'd seen her leading the tall flag girls onto Corsair Field, the marching band and girls drill team, blue and gold pom-pons in their hands, trailing behind, while Cooper stood on the sidelines with the other players, awaiting the playing of the national anthem and the opening kickoff.

Dan Cooper and Connie Bishop had dated for a while, well more than dated, but it had never developed, at least not the way Copper wanted. They didn't run in the same crowd, and it had taken a long time for Cooper to get over her. He was not sure he ever did.

He checked his watch and dialed the number.

"Cisco's." The voice was a man. Cooper could hear loud rock music in the background.

"Is there a Connie Bishop there?"

"Who wants to know?"

"I do."

"Look, pal, we're pretty busy here and I..."

"Is she there or not?"

"Yeah, she's here but she's busy serving drinks."

"Take this number down and have her call me when she gets a break."

"Yeah, yeah."

Cooper gave him his name and number. "What's your name?"

"Jerry."

"Thanks for your help, Jerry."

"Yeah, fuck you, pal."

Cooper got up and went into the bathroom and splashed cold water on his face. Back in the kitchen, he grabbed another beer out of the fridge and popped it open. He took a long pull then went back to the couch and waited.

Thirty minutes later the phone rang "This is Cooper."

"Danny? It's Connie Bishop."

He could still hear the music but it was muffled now, as if she had stepped outside. "Connie. What a surprise. It's been a long time. How are you?"

"Yeah, well, I'm okay. Just trying to keep my head above water. Not quite like the old days at Samohi."

"It's not for any of us." He sensed a nervousness in her voice. "Connie, I know you didn't call to go down memory lane. What's up?"

There was a pause, as if she were deciding how to begin. "You're the only cop I know." She paused again. "I'm being stalked, Danny."

"Stalked?"

"I guess that's what you'd call it. It's a guy I dated for a while. It got out of hand and I broke up with him. He's following me now, turns up everywhere I go. It's creepy and scaring me now."

"What's his name?"

"Ronnie Phillips. You remember him? He was in our class."

The name didn't register, but there were over six hundred in their senior class.

"He's a drummer. He played at our senior assembly."

Cooper searched his mind. He had a vague, hazy image of a dark haired kid flailing at his drums.

"He came in, here, where I work, at Cisco's. He recognized me. We talked a little and then he started showing up regularly, and we went out a few times. Nothing serious, but it didn't take long for me to realize it was a mistake. He wouldn't give up when I said it was over."

"How long?"

"Couple of months."

"Has he threatened you, made any physical moves, anything like that?"

"No, not really. He follows me home sometimes, parks near my apartment, and I think he's taken some pictures. I just want it to stop, and I wasn't sure what to do. Then I thought of you"

Cooper thought for a moment before he responded. "Look, Connie, I'm sure you know how it works. Unless he actually does something, the best you can do is file a report with the police, try to get a restraining order."

"But you are the police, Danny."

"I'm in robbery homicide, Connie. There's really nothing I can do." When she didn't say anything, he felt her disappointment.

"I know," she said quietly. "I just thought..."

"Look, you file a report and I'll verify that I know you, maybe move things along quicker, okay?"

"Thanks, Danny. I'd appreciate that. Sorry to bother you."

"Not a problem. Hey, maybe we could have coffee sometime, catch up on old times," he added.

"Sure," she said, but he could tell she knew it wouldn't happen. "I have to get back to work." Suddenly her voice brightened. "Hey, are you going to the class reunion?"

"I didn't know anything about it."

"It's next weekend. The first night is at Santa Monica Pier, at the Merry-Go-Round. They're going to have it catered by a hamburger chain."

"I don't know. I was never into that kind of thing."

"Well, at least think about it. I'll send you a flyer. It'll be fun and it would be great to see you again." There was a brief silence then, "If you go, call me when you get there."

"Well, no promises. You take care, Connie."

"I'll try."

Two

Thursday morning, Cooper logged on the computer and ran the name Ronnie (Ronald) Phillips. While waiting for the information to appear, he felt someone behind him. He turned to see Officer Tucker peering over his shoulder at the screen.

"New case, Lieutenant?"

"No, Tucker, just running a background check."

"Not much, just a couple of parking tickets. Photo from DMV."

Cooper looked at the screen. "Thanks, Tucker. Don't know what I'd do without you here to help me read."

Tucker's face turned red. "Sorry, Lieutenant. I just came over to give you this. Somebody dropped it off this morning." Tucker handed Cooper a folded sheet of paper.

"Thanks. Anything else?"

"No. Sorry to disturb you."

Tucker walked away as Cooper unfolded the paper. It was about the reunion, printed in blue and gold, Santa Monica's school colors, and promising a good time. At the bottom was a phone number and fee: one hundred dollars. Below that was a hand written note urging him to come, ending with several exclamation points and Connie Bishop's name.

Cooper leaned back and sighed. "What the hell," he mumbled, and dialed the number. The woman answering said in a perky voice he was late, but he could pay at the door. She took his name and promised he wouldn't be sorry. He didn't recognize her name nor she his.

He took out his own phone book and dialed another number. He leaned back in his chair and propped his feet on the desk.

"Hello."

"Is this the hottest woman in the FBI?"

"Coop?" Andie Lawrence said. Andie was the girl friend of his old friend jazz pianist Evan Horne.

"None other. Is Evan around?"

"He flew to L.A. this morning. He's got a three night gig down there. I'm sure he'll call you. Is this about a case?"

"No, nothing like that. Just trying to run down a guy.

Maybe a drummer. Thought Evan might know him."

"That's funny."

"What?"

"Evan is looking for a drummer, too."

"Seriously."

"Yeah. Evan played a concert at San Quentin recently. Thought he recognized this guy. According to Evan, he's a famous jazz drummer."

"I think my guy is a rocker and he's not in jail yet."

"Well, I can't help you there. I'll tell him you called if he doesn't call you."

"Okay, thanks, Andie."

"Coop."

"Yeah."

"We have to get together soon. It's been too long."

On the way to lunch, Cooper checked with the desk. Connie Bishop had filed a report. He read it but there was little more information than she'd given him on the phone.

"She was in early," the desk sergeant said. He looked at Cooper and smiled. "Not bad looking, too."

Cooper looked up from the report. "Yeah? Were you able to concentrate long enough to tell her how to file for a restraining order?"

"Sure was. Somebody you know?"

"High school classmate. Haven't seen her since."

The sergeant nodded. "I told her there wasn't much we could do."

"I'm sure you did."

He left the station and was halfway through a burger and fries when his cell phone rang.

"This is Cooper."

"I catch you at a donut shop?"

"Funny. I'm dining alfresco at an In-n-Out."

"How you doing? Andie told me you called. What's up?"

"With your extensive knowledge and contacts in the music world, have you heard of a drummer named Ronnie Phillips?"

"Doesn't ring a bell. He in some kind of trouble."

"He's been hassling a woman I knew in high school. Connie Bishop."

"Don't know her either."

"Well, you were only a lowly sophomore."

"Ah yes, you are much older. Lot of drummers in L.A. You might try the musicians union."

"Yeah, that's an idea. Why didn't I think of that?"

"Should I tell you?"

"Don't bother. Where are you playing?"

"At the Catalina, three nights. Going to come by?"

"Maybe. Listen my twenty-fifth high school reunion is Saturday night. Why don't you drop in? You can be my guest."

"How could I resist an offer like that? Where is it?"

"At the pier. Starts at five. You can still make your gig."

There's silence between them for a long moment. "I'll see," Evan said. "Anyway let's get together for lunch or something."

"I can do that."

Cooper studied the contents of his closet, trying to decide what would be appropriate attire for a high school reunion at Santa Monica Pier. There weren't a lot of choices. A few suits for work that could all stand a pressing, three sports coats, some slacks, and on a shelf, a stack of tee shirts and jeans. In the back, he found his letterman's jacket.

He'd earned it with two years on the football team as a rough and tumble linebacker. He held up the blue and gold jacket with the cream leather sleeves, gazed at it for a moment, remembering how excited he'd been that Connie Bishop had worn it for a few weeks as a sign they were going steady. He sighed, then hung it up again. Probably wouldn't fit anyway. He finally decided on jeans, a denim shirt, loafers and a brown suede jacket, one of his few indulgences.

He clipped his badge holder and gun on his belt and studied himself in the mirror. He shrugged, thinking this was going to be as good as it gets.

* * *

Santa Monica Pier was built in 1909. Sixteen hundred feet of concrete and wood pilings that today hosted over four million visitors annually, and was featured in countless movies and television shows. A campaign to tear down the pier in the 1970's was thwarted, but a storm in 1983 ravaged nearly a third of the structure. By 1990, it was rebuilt and now housed an amusement park, and scores of shops and restaurants.

Just after five, Cooper eased his dark blue Camaro down the steep incline and slowly drove past the Merry-Go-Round, taking in the large crowd of people milling about. He could hear the calliope-like music filtering out from inside. He continued on, and parked, got out and locked the car.

The pier had changed a lot since his high school days when he'd wandered along the boardwalk south of the pier, eating snow cones and corn dogs, stopping to watch the body builders groaning and sweating at Muscle Beach. Strolling down to the end of the pier, he let his mind roam over the many times he'd been here, some good, some bad. At the end, he leaned on the railing and gazed down at the water. It was still light and the sun on the horizon looked like half an orange.

He gripped the railing hard, remembering the night years ago when an insane killer had slashed his shoulder with a scalpel-like knife, the blood gushing as she raced from the scene, and Evan Horne kneeling over him, frantically calling 911.

He turned away and made his way back to the Carousel. There were more people now, all talking and smiling as they pushed inside. Two women he didn't recognize were seated at a table, crossing names off a list. They both looked up, studying his face.

"Dan Cooper," he said a little nervously and handed her a check.

"Of course," one of the women said. "Glad you could make it." She wrote his name on a white square name tag in marker pen and stuck it to his jacket. "Have fun."

The carousel was in full flight and the music was now almost deafening. He strolled around, scanning faces and name tags, but didn't see any he recognized. In one corner, he stopped at a machine that was dispensing Margaritas. He grabbed one of the plastic glasses, took a sip, and continued on, looking for Connie Bishop.

He suddenly felt a tug on his sleeve and turned to see a small, dark haired woman, her faced wreathed in a huge smile. "Oh my God, Dan Cooper."

He managed a glimpse of her name tag as she leaned in for a hug. He managed not to spill his drink as she pulled back and studied his face.

"Hello, Marcy."

"You don't remember me do you?"

"Well, it has been a long time."

"We were in history class for two semesters. I sat right behind you in Mr. Davis' class. Fifth period."

Cooper shrugged. "To tell you the truth, I—"

She laughed. "Just kidding. If it wasn't for name tags, we'd all be lost."

"I guess so. What have you been doing since those long ago days?"

She took a gulp of her drink. "Getting married, having kids. I have three. How about you?"

"None yet that I know of. Have you seen Connie Bishop?"

Marcy frowned. "I'm not sure I remember her. Was she your girlfriend?"

"Very briefly," Cooper said, wanting to move on.

"Well, happy hunting. I need another drink."

He watched her walk off, then continued circling the Carousel. He managed only a few steps when he heard his name called.

"Hey, Coop."

He turned and saw a face and name tag he recognized. John Winston grabbed his hand and pumped it. A slim fair woman stood next to him.

"This is the guy I was telling you about, honey. Remember, Coop, when you intercepted that pass against Hermosa Beach? Won us the game."

The woman with Winston stepped forward. "I'm John's wife," she said, taking Cooper's hand. "It's all he talks about."

Cooper remembered vividly. He'd jogged back to the sidelines and caught Connie Bishop clapping her hands and smiling at him for the first time.

"Nice to meet you," Cooper said to Winston's wife.

Winston grinned. "So what have you been up to? I've never seen you at one of these. I've made each one."

"I'm sure you have." Cooper caught a slight rolling of eyes from Winston's wife. "I'm still with the police."

"Police. You're a cop? Man, I never would have guessed."

"We all change, I guess." He felt his phone vibrating. "Excuse me." He pulled his phone out and flipped it open. "This is Cooper."

The Merry-Go-Round and music had stopped, but was now replaced by a small contingent of the current Samohi marching band. They trooped in and began playing the school song.

"Sorry," he said to Winston. "I have to take this."

Winston pointed to the band. "Doesn't that make you want to suit up again?"

"Not really." Cooper found a side exit that faced the boardwalk. "Say that again," he said into the phone. "I couldn't hear you."

"What the fuck was that? Sounded like a marching band." It was Sergeant Will Casey.

"It was a marching band. What's up?"

"We got one."

"Where?"

"On the beach. First lifeguard stand just north of the pier."

"I'll be right down. I'm on the pier now."

Three

Cooper crossed the parking lot and stepped onto the beach, walking as fast as he could in loafers, feeling the sand seep into his shoes. As he neared the lifeguard stand, Will Casey, dressed in jeans, a work shirt and dark blue wind breaker, broke away from the group of uniforms and techs, and met him.

"Hey, Will, what have we got?" It was not quite dark yet but two arc lights had been set up to illuminate the scene.

"White woman, mid-forties. Some kids found her." Casey looked toward the pier. "What were you doing up there?"

"High school reunion. Show me."

Someone had dragged three trash barrels over and strung the yellow crime scene tape around the lifeguard stand. Cooper and Casey ducked under the tape. The woman was almost face down in the sand. She was dressed in jeans, a dark sweatshirt, and some kind of running shoes. Her body was halfway under the overhang of the lifeguard stand.

Donald Ling, the Medical Examiner was kneeling down over her body, his hands encased in latex gloves. Ling was a small compact man, nearly bald, and wore wire rimmed glasses. He looked up at Cooper.

"Hello, Lieutenant. How goes it?"

"I've been better."

Ling brushed the woman's hair aside. "Two gunshots back of the head, no exit wounds. Looks like small caliber, probably twenty-two."

"Any I.D.?"

"Yeah." Ling held up a small wallet with a driver's license. Cooper glanced at the photo and name. He felt a tremor go through his body. "Turn her over."

Ling gently turned the body over and brushed the hair out of the woman's eyes.

"Shit," Cooper said.

"You know her?"

"Yeah. Connie Bishop."

"I thought maybe you did," Ling said. "Found this in her front pocket." He handed Cooper a plastic bag with a napkin inside. Cooper held it up to the light. Scribbled in black, on the Cisco's bar napkin was: Danny C, followed by Cooper's cell phone number.

He handed the baggy back to Ling. "We went to high school together. Time of death?"

Ling shrugged. "Couple of hours, maybe. I'll know more when I get her on the table."

Cooper checked his watch. It would have still been light then. Shot in broad daylight in the shadow of Santa Monica Pier? He looked at Will Casey. "Who found her?"

"Some kids. Guess they came down here for a make out session or maybe to watch the sunset." He pointed to the parking lot. "They're over there waiting."

Cooper nodded. "You question them already?"

"Yeah. They're pretty shook up."

"I can imagine. Okay, Will, make sure you get their contact numbers in case they remember something."

"Sure. So, how did the vic get your phone number?"

"She called me a few nights ago. Said a former boyfriend was stalking her, asked me to help out."

"And did you?"

"I told her to report it, file for a restraining order." Cooper glanced up at the pier. "I was going to meet her."

"All you could do," Casey said. "You okay?"

"Yeah, I guess." Cooper glanced again at Connie Bishop's body. He wanted to get out of there. "Can you finish up here?"

"Sure. Anything else?"

Cooper looked around. "Get a couple of uniforms and sift through the sand, say a fifteen foot diameter. Might find something."

"Got it."

Cooper glanced once again at Connie Bishop's body. "I'll handle the next of kin notification."

"Want some company?"

"No, better if I do it alone. I know her mother."

Cooper started to walk away, then stopped and turned back to Casey. "How many, Will?"

Casey smiled. "Thirty-seven days."

* * *

Cooper walked back across the beach to the pier and went up the steps to get his car. He eased past the Merry-Go-Round and up the incline to Ocean Avenue, and turned left heading north. He drove a few blocks then turned right on Montana Avenue, continuing east to 17th Street and turned left.

In Santa Monica, at least during Cooper's teenage years, Montana was the dividing line between moderately expensive homes and very expensive homes. But Montana was more than a real estate line. During his high school years, it also represented a cultural boundary, a symbolic divider that separated one crowd from another. Connie Bishop had lived north of Montana. Cooper had lived south of Santa Monica Boulevard.

Three blocks up 17th Street, Cooper pulled to the curb in front of a mock English Tudor home. He shut off the engine, and looked at the house. It hadn't changed a bit. Same neatly trimmed lawn, same array of flowers and shrubs under the windows, lit now by floodlights. It had been years, but Cooper had been to this home many times. Now, he didn't want to get out of the car.

Dan Cooper loved being a cop, and he'd done it all. Black and white patrol cars, motor cycles, even a stint on helicopters before applying for detectives. That had meant burglary, robbery, and finally homicide as he moved up the ladder. But tonight, this was every cop's worst case scenario. He'd made next of kin notification scores of times but never to someone he had once known. Breaking the news to a woman he knew that her daughter had been shot, murdered execution style. He let out a long sigh and got out of the car.

He walked up to the front door and rang the bell. When the door opened, he looked at Connie Bishop's mother, Marion. She was a tall slim woman, her grayish hair cut short. She blinked at Cooper and put her hand to her mouth. She glanced over his shoulder, as if looking for someone behind him. He'd seen her do that once before. He'd taken Connie to a party and it had gotten out of hand. She'd drunk way too much, got sick, and was scared to face her mother.

"Danny?"

"Hello, Marion." She was in slippers, a dressy pale blue robe, and glasses on a gold chain around her neck.

She blinked again and suddenly her eyes pooled with tears as if she already knew why he was there.

"I'm sorry, Marion. It's bad news."

She put her hand to her mouth and leaned against the doorway. Cooper stepped forward and took her by the shoulders. "Let's go inside." He pushed the door shut and guided her into the living room and eased her down on a curved white sofa facing a large flat screen television, the sound turned down low on a CNN news show.

She wiped her eyes and looked up him. "There's no mistake?"

Cooper shook his head. "No, Marion. It was Connie."

"You were there?"

"Yes." He pulled an ottoman close and sat down facing her.

She leaned over and covered her face with her hands. Her body shook with sobs, her breath coming fast. Cooper could only watch. He turned around and switched off the television.

Finally, she sat up and reached for a box of tissues on a side table and wiped her eyes. She looked up at Cooper. "Was it an accident?"

Cooper sighed, and plunged ahead, thinking it better to be frank, get it over with. "No, Marion. Connie was shot." She met his gaze and he saw all the questions in her eyes. How? Where? When? Why?

"At the beach, near Santa Monica Pier. We're not sure yet what happened. She was found about an hour ago. We'll know more when the ME examines her."

Marion let out a low moan. "Shot? Oh my God, Danny..."

"I know," Cooper said. "Can I get you some water or something."

"Yes, please." She leaned back against the sofa as Cooper got up and went into the kitchen. He brought a glass of water back. She was sitting up now, a tissue clutched in her hand. She took the water, drank deeply, then set the glass on the table.

"I'll have to... to identify her won't I?" She started to get up. "Should we go now?"

"There's no hurry," Cooper said, then realizing what he'd said. "I made the tentative identification, but officially you'll have to do it." He waited a few moments, letting her settle down a little.

"I know this is difficult, but I need to ask you some questions first."

"Questions?" She stared at him for a moment. "What kind of questions?"

He caught himself before saying just routine. There was nothing routine about questioning the victim's mother about her daughter's murder. "When did you last see Connie?"

"About a week ago. She came by, we had coffee. It was just one of her rare, periodic visits to check in with me."

"Did she mention a man named Ron Phillips?"

Marion shrugged. "Not that time, but she told me she'd been seeing him. Why?"

"She called me a few nights ago. She said he'd been following her. Apparently, she'd broken it off but he started following her, taking photos. She wanted to know what I, what the police could do."

"Do you think he did it?"

"We don't know yet, Marion. It's too early to tell."

"She was very guarded with me over the past few months. I couldn't get her to talk much." She cast her eyes down. "It's been a long time since we were really close, like before."

"Do you know if she was in any trouble, something financial maybe?"

Marion shook her head. "No, I knew something was wrong, but I just couldn't get her to open up." She looked away for a moment. "And now I'll never know if there was something I could have done."

"I'm sorry to ask this, Marion, but what about drugs?"

She shook her head. "No, at least I don't think so. After the divorce, she was just kind of lost."

Cooper nodded. "What kind of car did Connie have?"

"I think it was a Honda, a few years old."

"And did she have a cell phone?"

"Yes. Do you need the number?"

"Yes, that would be helpful." He handed her a pen and a small notebook from his jacket pocket and watched her scribble down the number. "I think that's it for now. Are you up to going down to the..." He couldn't bring himself to say morgue.

"Up to identifying the body of my murdered daughter?" Her words came out harshly, then she quickly recovered. "I'm sorry, Danny. I didn't mean to sound like that." She stood up and Cooper put his arm around her shoulders.

"We can do it in the morning if you want."

"No, I want to go now. I need to see her. Let me get dressed, get my coat."

"One more thing. Do you have a key to her apartment? I need your permission to have a look around. Maybe I'll find something that can lead us to who and why."

"Of course." She left him standing and went off to her bedroom.

Cooper walked over to a gleaming baby grand piano. The lid was down and several framed photos were arranged on top. He picked one up of Connie in a cap and gown. He was still staring at it when Marion came back, her coat on over slacks and a sweater, her face washed.

"That was taken when she graduated from UCLA. She was a beautiful girl," she said.

"Yes, she was."

"She had her whole life ahead of her then."

She moved closer, as Cooper returned the photo to the piano. He turned to her and held her for a moment, feeling the tremors in her body.

He stepped back. "The key?"

"I'll have to look for it," she said.

"Marion, please don't go there before I've had a look."

"I won't. I promise."

Cooper nodded. "Thank you. It's just that..."

"I understand. You don't have to explain."

She tried for a smile but didn't quite make it.

"I'm glad it was you, Danny," she said.

"So am I."

They drove in silence to the coroner's for the identification. Cooper glanced at Marion Bishop several times, but she kept her eye straight ahead. He stood with her in front of the viewing window while a tech drew the sheet back, revealing Connie Bishop's face. She looked peaceful, as if she were asleep, Cooper thought. Not a mark on her face, and seeing her, even in the stark, unforgiving light, he realized how little Connie Bishop had changed.

Marion stared through the glass, nodded and turned to Cooper. "Yes, that's my daughter, Connie Bishop," she said.

He drove her home, and offered to call someone to stay with her, but she'd declined.

"No, Danny, I need some time alone. Don't bother Jack. I'll call him myself."

"If you think that's best," Cooper said. He didn't think it was, letting her former husband know their daughter had been murdered, but he let it go.

He took her to the door. She started inside, then stopped. "Wait a minute." She disappeared for a couple of minutes then came back and handed Cooper a key. "I just remembered where it was."

"Thanks," Cooper said. "I'll get this back to you."

A preview of the new Evan Horne mystery

So Beautiful, So Dead
Robert J. Randisi

Val O'Farrell looked down at the dead girl with a gut wrenching sadness. So beautiful, so dead.

"What a body, huh? Why would anyone want to cancel the ticket of a babe like that? And pluggin' her in the head, too. Jeez, how you gonna figure that?"

O'Farrell turned to look at Detective Sam McKeever.

"What?" McKeever asked. "She's a babe. Hey, she's lyin' there naked under a sheet, what am I supposed to do, not look?"

"No," O'Farrell said, "she's used to bein' looked at."

"Like most beautiful young dames, huh?"

"This one more than some," O'Farrell said. "She's supposed to be one of the contestants at that new Beauty Pageant out in Jersey."

"Yeah? No kiddin'?" McKeever said. "I heard they was gonna let them wear these new skin tight bathing suit things."

"Tight and skimpy."

"You seen 'em?"

"Not yet."

During the beauty pageant in Washington, D.C. last year, the contestants had worn long stockings and tunic bathing suits. However, Atlantic City's first contest was going to be something really different and special because the censors had seen fit to lift their bans on bare knees and skin tight suits. It remained to be seen if the idea would fly.

"Hey," McKeever said, "you better get out of here before the boss shows up. You ain't a cop no more, you know."

"Oh, I know."

O'Farrell had retired from the force two years ago, in 1919, and had opened his own detective agency. He'd been on the "inside" so often, though, while on the job that he catered to a pretty high class clientele, these days. He went from being the best dressed cop in town to the best dressed shamus.

"How'd you know to come up here, anyway?" McKeever asked.

"I was supposed to pick her up and take her out to Jersey."

"You knew her?"

"Yeah."

"Maybe you better tell me about it, Val," McKeever said, folding his arms, and O'Farrell did. He laid it out for the detective just as it had happened...

2

Vincent Balducci had come into his office two days before with flash and confidence bordering on arrogance. Most of the flash came from the sparks he was wearing in a couple of rings.

"I've got a job for you, Mr. O'Farrell," he'd said, after introducing himself. He said his name like O'Farrell was supposed to know who he was. He did, but he didn't tip his hand—not yet.

"How did you get my name, Mr. Balducci?"

"You were referred to me by a mutual acquaintance," Balducci said. "His name is not important. He said you used to be a cop, an honest cop—or as honest as they get around here. He said you were thorough and you wouldn't gouge me on your fee just because I'm rich." Balducci looked around O'Farrell's well-furnished office. "I'm thinkin' the last part is probably right."

"All the parts are right, Mr. Balducci," O'Farrell said. "Why don't we get to the point of the visit?" O'Farrell motioned him to his visitor's chair.

"All right." Vincent Balducci said, seating himself. He laid his coat over his lap. O'Farrell noticed it had a velvet collar. He laid a matching hat atop it. His hair was dark—too dark to be natural—and shiny, combed straight back. "Yes, why don't we? Do you know who I am?"

100

"I read the newspaper," O'Farrell said. The year-old *New York Times* already had an archive of stories on Vincent Balducci, a millionaire "philanthropist." What that generally meant to O'Farrell was that the man had a lot of money and didn't know what to do with it.

"That will save us some time, then," Balducci said.

That was when Balducci told O'Farrell about Georgie Taylor. He was married, he said, but it was a loveless, sexless marriage that was entered into for convenience. Naturally he needed a friend outside his marriage. When he met Georgie he knew she was the one.

"But she's younger, right?" O'Farrell asked.

"Uh, well, yes," Balducci said, "quite a bit younger. I am sixty-five and she is, uh, twenty-five."

"You look good," O'Farrell said. "I had you pegged for fifty-five."

"Thank you," Balducci said, "I try to keep myself in shape."

And he did a fine job. Except for his obviously dyed hair and some lines on his face, he did look younger than he was. He was tall, fit, and he moved like a younger man. O'Farrell sneaked a look at his own growing paunch. He was fifteen years younger than the millionaire, but they probably looked the same age. He decided not to think about that.

"Lots of married men have dames on the side, Mr. Balducci," he said to the man. "Where do I come in?"

"Have you heard about this beauty pageant in Atlantic City this weekend?"

"I heard something about it," O'Farrell said. "Is that the one with the new bathing suits?"

"Yes," Balducci said. "One of the major sponsors is the Atlantic City Businessman's League, of which I am a member."

O'Farrell was starting to get the drift, but he let the man go on.

"I've entered Georgie in the pageant."

"You didn't guarantee she'd win, did you?" O'Farrell asked. "You're not going to tell me that the fix is in, are you?"

"Uh, no," Balducci said, "that, uh, that part is not your concern."

So maybe the fix was in. But okay, the client is always right. That wasn't his concern.

"Fine."

"Georgie is very beautiful, and talented, and she has a big career ahead of her."

O'Farrell almost asked, "As what?" but bit his tongue.

"But I think she might be in danger."

"From who?"

"Well... an old boyfriend, other contestants... my wife..."

"Does your wife know about Georgie?"

"Not exactly. She knows that I have... friends on the side, but she doesn't know about Georgie... specifically."

"All right," O'Farrell said, "go on."

"The contest kicks off with a gala event taking place at the Atlantic City Yacht Club on Friday. Among others, my wife will be there. I want you to escort Georgie."

"Be her date?"

"Er, as it were, yes—and protect her."

"We've never met—"

"I will take you to her apartment on Beekman Place for an introduction," Balducci said. "After that it will be up to the two of you to plan your Friday evening."

"Mr. Balducci," O'Farrell said, "today is already Wednesday and I haven't got a thing to wear."

"On top of a thousand dollar free," Balducci said, taking the comment completely serious, "I will buy you a new wardrobe and pay all other expenses for the night. I would send you to my tailor, but there's no time, so you can simply shop in the best men's stores available."

O'Farrell was a man who enjoyed good clothes. He knew where to shop. Even while still in the employ of the New York City Police Department he used to dress better than any other detective—regardless of rank—leading to speculation that he was on the take. It was only the fact that everyone knew how scrupulously honest he was that kept anyone from believing that.

"All right," O'Farrell said. "When and where do I meet the

young, uh, lady?"

"Tonight, if you're free," Balducci said. He leaned forward and placed a slip of paper on the desk. "Come to that address and eight p.m. I'll make the introductions."

O'Farrell leaned forward and picked up the paper, glanced at it, then put it in his shirt pocket.

"I'll need an advance."

"Of course," Balducci said. He took a wad of cash out of his pocket. No checks, no paper trail.

"Five hundred now? And a hundred for clothes?"

"Better make it two for clothes," O'Farrell said.

Balducci didn't hesitate. He peeled off seven one hundred dollar bills and placed them on O'Farrell's desk.

"Will that do?"

"That's fine." O'Farrell left the cash where it was.

"I'll see you tonight, then."

"I have some more questions."

Balducci stood up. He shot his cuffs and looked at his watch. "I'll answer the rest of your questions tonight. Right now I have another appointment."

O'Farrell walked his new client to the door.

"Eight o'clock, then," Balducci said, and left.

After Balducci was gone O'Farrell picked up the seven one hundred dollar bills and rubbed them together. He turned and looked out his second floor window down to Fifth Avenue, where a chauffeur was holding the back door of a Rolls Royce open for Vincent Balducci. He probably should have asked for more money. A guy who rides in a Rolls and is dizzy for a young dame probably wouldn't have squawked about it.

3

O'Farrell presented himself at the Beekman Place address at seven fifty-five. He paused out front to look up at the place. It was only five stories, but Beekman Place was not an inexpensive address. Each apartment was occupied by money—or, as in this case, paid for by someone with money.

He was wearing one of the new suits he'd bought that afternoon. It was September and the weather was still mild so he'd bought one brown linen and one blue pinstriped. He was wearing the linen. The pinstriped was for the night at the Yacht Club.

The young doorman announced him and he was allowed up to the third floor. When he rang the doorbell the door was opened by Balducci, himself. O'Farrell had been expecting a butler, or at least, a maid.

"Come in," the man said. "Georgie is still getting dressed."

O'Farrell entered and closed the door behind him. He followed Balducci down a short hall until they entered a plushly furnished living room.

"I've made a pitcher of martinis," his host said. "Would you like one?"

"Sure."

"Olive or onion?"

"Olive, please."

Balducci poured out two martinis, put olives in both, and then handed one to O'Farrell.

"I was expecting a servant to answer the door," the detective said. "Maid's night off?"

"No servants," Balducci said. "It's bad enough the doorman knows me and see me coming here."

O'Farrell understood.

"Ah," Balducci said, looking past him, "here's Georgie now."

O'Farrell turned. He didn't know what he'd expected to see, but Georgie took his breath away. She was tall and slender, but with a proud thrust of breasts. Her dark hair was piled high atop her head, leaving her pale shoulders bare in a powder blue gown that bared both shoulders, but was high-necked. Since 1919 hems had been rising and, currently, it was not unheard of for them to be six inches from the floor—affording a nice view of ankle—but Georgie's gown was full length. It was her eyes, however, that really got O'Farrell. They were violet, the most amazing color he'd ever seen, and they were great big eyes. When she blinked, he thought he could feel it inside.

She was pretty enough to be a Ziegfeld girl. O'Farrell wondered why Balducci didn't just use his pull to get her that job, rather than put her in some silly pageant?

"Georgie, this is Val O'Farrell, the private detective I hired to protect you."

"To hide me, you mean," she said, tightly. She was smoking a cigarette, took a moment to remove a bit of tobacco from her tongue with her thumb and pinky while appraising O'Farrell. Flashes of light on her fingers attested to the fact that Balducci didn't mind sharing his love of diamonds. He still had his rings on. "Well, he's big enough for me to hide behind."

"I just want him to protect you, darling," Balducci said.

O'Farrell suddenly realized how dressed up the two of them were and what it meant. Balducci's suit easily cost five times what his own new suit cost.

"Are you folks going out to dinner?" he asked.

"We all are," Balducci said. "I thought it would be a good opportunity for us to get acquainted."

"Don't let him fool you, Mr. Detective," Georgie said. "He just wants to use you as a beard, that way if anyone sees us together he can say I was your date. He's become an expert at hiding me."

"Georgie..."

"Oh, all right," she said, "I'll be a nice girl. Mr. O'Farrell, would you care to join us for dinner?"

"Well, I don't—"

"Please," she said. "Vincent will be paying the bill."

"Well," O'Farrell agreed, "when you put it that way..."

The only chink in Georgie Jenskin's beautiful armor was her voice. It was high pitched, almost a whine, and marred what was otherwise a perfect picture. O'Farrell knew nothing about how this beauty pageant was supposed to be run. He wondered if it called for the girls to actually speak?

Dinner was a tense affair at a nearby restaurant that O'Farrell suspected was below Balducci's usual dining standards. Even Georgie had lifted one side of her lips and sniffed when they entered. For his part, O'Farrell found his steak delicious.

For a dinner where they were supposed to be getting acquainted—actually, he and Georgie—Vincent Balducci did most of the talking. O'Farrell spent more time looking at Georgie than listening to his client.

Later, when they returned to the apartment house on Beekman Place, Balducci stopped in the lobby and said, "I'm not coming up."

"Why not?" Georgie asked.

"Because you two need to talk," Balducci said. "I want you to spend some time together and really talk, this time." He turned to face O'Farrell. "Georgie has all the details about the party at the Yacht Club Friday night. I won't see you again until then. I'll, uh, have my wife with me, so if we come face to face we will just be meeting. Do you understand?"

"Perfectly."

"My dear," Balducci said. He leaned over to kiss Georgie but she imperiously presented him with nothing but a cheek. "I'll see you soon."

"Yes," she said, quietly. Then she looked at O'Farrell. "Well, come on, then."

The building had an elevator, but Georgie preferred to walk, which O'Farrell had discovered on their way down. He, in fact, had a distrust of elevators and had walked up when he first arrived. This was something he had shared with his friend, the great Bat Masterson. Masterson, a legend of the old west, now lived in New York and not only had a column in *The Morning Telegraph*, but was a vice president of the newspaper. In his mid-sixties, the old western lawman still had more faith in a horse than an elevator, and almost never used a telephone if he didn't have to. O'Farrell liked to think of himself as someone who had been born too late. He should have been with Bat on the streets of Dodge City, with a gun on his hip.

Georgie opened her door with her key and marched right to the sideboard. She was dragging her mink stole behind her and just let it drop to the floor. O'Farrell bent, picked it up and deposited it on a chair.

"I need a drink," she said. "Join me?"

"Why not, but if you don't mind I'll have bourbon."

"A man after my own heart," she said. She poured bourbon over some ice cubes in two glasses and handed him one. She sipped herself, clunked the glass against her teeth and eyed him over the rim.

"After this we could go to the bedroom and fuck our brains out," she offered. "Or we could take the drinks with us and go in now."

"Somehow," O'Farrell said, "I don't think that's what your boyfriend had in mind when he said he wanted us to get better acquainted."

"You don't think so?" she asked, raising her eyebrows. "Why else do you think he sent us up here alone? Come on, I saw the way you were lookin' at me in the restaurant."

"We're supposed to talk about Friday night," he said, "about the beauty pageant."

"Beauty pageant," she said. She held her glass tightly and let her other arm swing loosely about. He didn't remember how many drinks she'd had at dinner, but she certainly seemed drunk now. "What a crock! What a stupid idea. Marching around in bathing suits while a bunch of lecherous old men decide who the winner will be."

"I wasn't aware that the contest would be judged by a panel of old men?"

"Oh, it's not, but you know what I mean." She finished her drink and poured herself another.

"You don't think you can win?"

She turned around quickly, sloshing some bourbon onto her wrist. She took a moment to lick it off, a move O'Farrell found particularly erotic, especially since she kept those violet eyes on him the whole time. He shifted his legs, his position in his chair, but it didn't help.

"Of course I can win," she said. "I've got the looks, don't you think?"

"Oh, definitely."

"I just don't have the voice," she said, candidly. "I'm no dummy, I just sound like one. I know that when the contestants start to speak—to answer questions—my voice is going to be a liability."

O'Farrell was impressed. The girl had no illusions about

herself or, apparently, her situation.

"And Vincent doesn't love me," she said. She wiggled the fingers of one hand at him, the light playing off the sparks. "He owns me, like one of these diamonds. It sounds odd. He just wants to have me on his arm to show me off, but then he never takes me out. I can't explain it. All I know is he's not here tonight and I really want it. Whataya say?"

"Look, Georgie—"

She did something with the top of her dress and it fell to her waist. Her breasts were beautiful round orbs with tight pink nipples. She would not have made a good Ziegfeld girl, after all. Too big. She stared at him with those big violet eyes and poured the rest of her bourbon over her bare chest. One ice cube fell to the floor while another disappeared into her dress.

Why not? he thought, coming to his feet. When would he ever get a chance like this again? He had to find out where that second ice cube had gone.

4

They spent the next morning getting acquainted over breakfast because they really didn't do much talking during the night. When O'Farrell asked her about the doorman she told him not to worry. The doorman liked her and wouldn't say a word to Balducci about O'Farrell staying the entire night.

"So who would want to hurt you?" he asked her over steak and eggs at a diner around the corner. He was wearing his linen suit again, but had left the silk tie off this morning, preferring to stow it in his jacket pocket. Georgie was wearing an angora sweater with a pin in the shape of the letter "G", and a skirt with a fashionable six-inch hem. The sweater molded itself to her breasts. Her golden hair was pulled back in a ponytail. She wasn't wearing as much make up as the night before and looked much younger. But those eyes... made up or not, they popped.

"That's another one of Vincent's fantasies," she said. "Nobody wants to hurt me. I don't need a bodyguard—

although I certainly needed you last night, didn't I?" She ran her toe up his leg.

"Just answer the question and stop playing footsie under the table, young lady."

"Ooh, Daddy," she purred, "scold me some more."

Somehow, after spending the night with her, her voice didn't seem quite as whiney or annoying. She certainly had more than enough other qualities to make up for it—although some of those qualities certainly would not be seen by the judges.

"Georgie," O'Farrell said, moving his leg, "be serious."

"I am serious," she said. "Nobody wants to hurt me. Vincent thinks everyone wants what he's got. Well, if no one knows he's got me, what's the problem?"

"Someone must know," O'Farrell said. "Somebody who works for him but knows when to make excuses for him."

"Sure, they know he's got someone," she said, "but not who it is."

"Look," O'Farrell said, "Balducci is paying me to protect you, and that's what I'm going to do."

"And more, I think," she said.

After breakfast O'Farrell walked Georgie back to her building and said he had to go home to change.

"Aren't you afraid someone's gonna attack me?"

"I think what Vincent wants is for me to escort you to the beauty pageant, and protect you," O'Farrell said, "starting with the party at the Yacht Club. So I'll pick you up here— what time is the party?"

"The festivities start at three," she said. "I'm supposed to be there at noon, though."

"Noon?"

"I'm part of the show, after all," she said, archly.

"How many contestants are there?"

"There were supposed to be a lot, but we ended up with just twelve. Some folks—sponsors—are really upset about it."

"Twelve beautiful girls, huh?" O'Farrell said. "All right, then I guess I'll pick you up here at ten. I assume Balducci will supply transportation?"

"He'll have an automobile here to take us over to New Jersey. Probably a Rolls."

O'Farrell made a face. He still preferred horses, but it was a long way to Atlantic City.

"Okay," he said. "I'll see you then."

"What about tomorrow?" she asked. "Don't you want to see me tomorrow?"

"I don't think—"

She came closer to him.

"After everything we did to each other last night you can wait two days to see me?"

"Hey, Georgie," O'Farrell said, "you're the one who said what we did last night was just sex."

"Well, yes," she said, touching his lapel, "but it was good sex, wasn't it?"

"It was great," he said, "fabulous. You're a wonderful gal, but you belong to my client."

"That didn't seem to bother you last night?"

"Last night I gave in to bourbon and a pair of gorgeous... eyes"

She smiled. "You think my... eyes are gorgeous?" she asked, pausing suggestively exactly where he did.

"You know they are." Behind Georgie, O'Farrell could see the doorman watching him. A different one today than last night, but another young man, this one eyeing Georgie appreciatively—not that O'Farrell could blame him.

"You sure this doorman is not on Balducci's payroll?"

"I'm this sure," she said. She slid her hands around his neck and gave him a kiss that could have melted the soles of his shoes. Her tongue fluttered in his mouth and she bit his bottom lip lightly before stepping back and smiling at him.

"Okay," she said, wiggling her fingers at him, "see you the day after tomorrow, Lover."

5

But Friday, when he went to pick her up, there was no answer at the door. He went down to ask the doorman if he'd seen Georgie Taylor that morning. This was the same doorman who had watched her kiss him goodbye the other day.

"No, sir," the man said. "I haven't seen her today, at all."

O'Farrell studied the man for a moment, then took a ten out of his wallet.

"What's your name?"

"Henry, sir." Henry was a young man in his late twenties. He was eyeing the ten in O'Farrell's hand hungrily.

"Tell me, Henry, has Miss Taylor had any visitors since I was here?"

"No, sir."

"Not Mr. Balducci?"

"Well, yes sir," Henry said. "He came by last night. I didn't know you meant him."

"Did he stay the night?"

"No, sir," Henry said, "He left after a few hours."

"Okay... anyone else?"

"No, sir," the doorman said. "She hasn't had anyone else upstairs since you left the other morning—uh, except for Mr. Balducci."

"Did she go out at all since then?"

"Oh, yes, sir," Henry said. "I saw her go out yesterday. She did some shopping and came home with a few bags. She stayed in after that—at least, as long as I was on duty."

"How many doormen are there, Henry?"

"Three, sir," Henry said, "but only one other—Leslie—" he said the name with a wry grin, "has been on duty since you were here. He worked yesterday afternoon and evening as well as the, uh, evening you arrived."

"I'd like to find out what he knows, Henry," O'Farrell said.

"I could ask him when I see him."

"No," O'Farrell said, "I'd like to find out as soon as possible. Could you call him? There'd be ten in it for him, and a second ten for you."

The promise of twenty bucks sent Henry to the phone to call Leslie. He asked the second doorman the same questions O'Farrell had asked him, and hung up shaking his head.

"Leslie says he never saw anyone go up to Miss Taylor's apartment, and he never saw her leave."

O'Farrell went over it in his head. So she'd only been out once all day Thursday, didn't go out at all anymore on Wednesday when he left her, or any time Friday morning until now. Balducci was the only person seen going up.

"Is there a back door, Henry?"

"Yes, sir," the doorman said. "It's kept locked. Tenants don't use it, and don't have a key. Its access to an alley where we throw out the trash, sometimes take deliveries."

"So you have a key, in case of deliveries."

"Yes, sir."

"Any deliveries since I left here Wednesday morning?" O'Farrell asked.

"No, sir."

O'Farrell gave Henry the twenty dollars and then took out another twenty.

"Henry, have you got a key to Miss Taylor's apartment?"

"Yes, sir," the doorman said. "Do you think something's happened to her?"

"Let's just say I have a bad feeling."

Henry waved away the second twenty and got the key...

"We found her like this," he told McKeever.

"Well, you've got each other to vouch for that," the detective said. "Is there anything you haven't told me?"

There was. He'd left out the part about having sex with his client's girl, and spending the note. He only hoped Henry had left that part out, too.

"No, that's it."

"That pretty much jibes with what the doorman told us. Well, you better scram, Val. The Lieutenant's gonna show up soon and he ain't gonna like it if—"

"Too late," the police officer on the door said.

O'Farrell and McKeever both turned in to see Lieutenant Mike Turico enter the room.

"Well, well," Turico said when he saw O'Farrell. "Guess you musta forgot you ain't a cop no more, O'Farrell."

"Hello, Mike."

Turico approached O'Farrell and felt the texture of wide lapel of the private detective's blue pin striped suit...

"Turnin' private musta really paid off for you, Val," he said. He looked down at the matching fedora O'Farrell was holding.

"I'm doin' okay, Mike," O'Farrell said, "Thanks for askin'."

"Bet the swells really like you in this outfit." He touched O'Farrell's red silk tie, straightening it. Without looking at McKeever he asked, "Who let him in here?"

"He just walked in, boss," the detective said. "You know how Val is."

"Yeah," Turico said, "I do." He stepped back from O'Farrell, jerked his thumb at the door and said, "Blow."

"Nice to see you again, too, Mike," O'Farrell said. The two had not gotten along when they were both police detectives, and it was no different now. Turico had always resented how O'Farrell got the high profile cases, but O'Farrell had a reputation forgetting results, and Turico didn't. Naturally, Turico had risen to the rank of Lieutenant, since rank had more to do with who you knew than getting results.

Turico moved to inspect the body and McKeever followed O'Farrell to the door.

"Sam, sorry to bust in on you like this."

McKeever waved his apology off.

"Forget it. If the boss is gonna chew me out it's gonna be over this or somethin' else. But just between you and me, Val, you got a personal interest in this?"

"My client pays the bills for this place," O'Farrell said. "I met the girl. I liked her."

"Ah," McKeever said, "the sugar daddy. You got an idea where I can find him?"

"You can get his address from the manager of the building," O'Farrell said. "I don't have it on me. And he's got an office downtown somewhere. If the manager can't help you, let me know."

"McKeever," Lieutenant Turico yelled, "get your ass over

here."

"Gotta go, Val. You gonna look into this?"

"I'm not sure, Sam."

"Well, let me know, huh?" McKeever said. "Turico might be here, but this is my case."

"I'll stay in touch." As he went out past the uniformed policeman he patted his arm and said, "See you, Ed."

Did he have a personal interest? Goddamn right, he did.

6

O'Farrell was still dressed for the Yacht Club party when he approached Bat Masterson at his desk at *The Morning Telegraph.* The old lawman turned newspaperman made a show of covering his eyes.

"I'm blind! I'm blind!" he cried, then dropped his hands. "Damned if you ain't the prettiest man I ever did see, O'Farrell."

"Cut it, Bat," O'Farrell said. "You're not the only one who can get all duded up."

"'All duded up'?" Bat asked. "I don't think I've heard anyone say that since Wyatt Earp back in ninety-nine."

O'Farrell rushed on, afraid his friend would start telling one of his stories which would end with him taking a replica of his old gun out of his desk drawer. O'Farrell usually enjoyed Bat's stories, but he had no time for them today.

"Bat," O'Farrell said, sitting down across from his friend, "what's the skinny on the beauty pageant out in Atlantic City."

Bat sat back and smiled broadly. Approaching his late sixties both his waist and his face had filled out some, but when he smiled like that it took years off him.

"I know I'm one of the judges," he said.

"How'd you get that job?"

"Hell, they just up and asked me," the old gunman said. "Who am I to say no to judging a bevy of beauties?"

"Who asked you?"

"Some fella from the—what's it called—Atlantic City something—"

"—Businessman's League?"

"That's it. Said they needed artists to judge and I qualified 'cause I'm a writer. You believe that? I never been called an artist before."

"Or a writer."

"You want me to shoot you?"

"Sorry."

"What's your interest?"

"I'll tell you," O'Farrell said, "but you've got to keep it under your hat for a while."

"That's a hard thing to ask a newspaperman to do, Val, but okay. For you I'll do it."

O'Farrell fed him the whole story, and Bat listened in complete silence...

"What do you want me to do?" Bat asked.

"I wanted to find out what you knew about Balducci, and about the pageant."

"Like what?"

"Like are they on the up-and-up, both of them?"

"As far as I know the pageant is," Bat said.

"Does that mean that Balducci isn't?"

"There's been talk that Balducci is in bed with a, uh, certain criminal element."

"Like what?"

"Well, some of the crime reporters have been wondering if he's in with this new mafia," Bat said. "They wonder if he's not involved with the giggle juice trade and other illegal activities."

"You sound like you're being real careful with your language. Why would a rich man like him want to run liquor with the mob?"

"Well," Bat said, "this new breed of—what do they call 'em—gangsters is a lot different from the bad guys of my day. You can't tell by white hats and black hats anymore, Val. And who knows why rich men do what rich men do?"

"Okay, so Balducci might be in bed with the mafia," O'Farrell said, "but the pageant is on the level?"

"As far as I can tell," Bat said. "I wouldn't have agreed to be a judge if I thought different."

"How are you getting out there?"

"They're sending a car for me."

"What time?"

"Around five, I think. Do you want to ride with me?" Bat asked.

"Yes, I would," O'Farrell said. "I think if I walk in with you I'll be able to get around easier."

"Fine," Bat said, "meet me here around quarter to five and we'll go look at some girls. What will you be doing until then?"

O'Farrell stood up. "Trying to find my client before the police do."

7

O'Farrell knew more about the mafia and Johnny Torrio—which were natural offshoots of Paul Kelly and his Five Points Gang—then he wanted to let on to Bat Masterson. Friend or no friend, it wasn't wise to let a newspaperman know all that you knew. However, he'd met Vincent Balducci and didn't see him as a gangster. It was more likely he had some connections—crooked and lucrative—to Tammany Hall.

O'Farrell was unable to locate Balducci that morning and into the afternoon. He wondered if the police were having the same problem? At least he knew the man was supposed to be at the Yacht Club in Jersey that evening.

He decided to make one more stop before meeting Bat Masterson to go to New Jersey. There were still some things he needed to know, and his buddy Sam McKeever would have the answers.

O'Farrell had decided not to change his clothes after leaving Bat Masterson, so when he returned to the offices of *The Morning Telegraph* he was still dressed for the Yacht Club party.

He met Bat in front of the building as a boxy, yellow

Pierce Arrow Roadster pulled up. He and Bat got in and the driver pulled away and headed for New Jersey.

"Find your man?' Bat asked.

"No."

"Think he's in hidin'?"

"I doubt it," O'Farrell said. "Men with his money—and his connections—rarely go into hiding, even if they are suspected of murder."

"And is he?"

"He's on the list," the detective said, "since he was paying the bills for the girl."

"And what's your interest in this, Val, other than him bein' your client?"

"I met the girl and liked her, Bat," O'Farrell said. "She shouldn't have died like that."

"Like what?" Bat asked. "If you told me how she died I forgot."

"She was shot, once, in the temple."

"Any chance of suicide?"

"The word I got from the cops was that she was shot from close range, but there was no gun at the scene."

"Well, that rules out suicide—unless someone removed the gun."

"Too complicated," O'Farrell said. "I've found, in my experience, the simplest answer is usually the right one. Once you start factoring in 'what ifs' you just complicate things, and muddy the waters."

"What about the gangster angle?"

"That muddies the waters," O'Farrell said, as if it was a perfect example of what he had been talking about. "I'm looking for a clean, simple solution."

"You're gonna solve this thing?"

"Bat," O'Farrell said, "I think I already have."

When they pulled up in front of the Yacht Club there were many other vehicles arriving, as well as those which had already arrived. More Pierce Arrows, Rolls Royce's, even some sporty Stutz Roadsters.

O'Farrell and Bat were dropped right in front of the Club. A tent had been erected nearby to accommodate all the guests for party, and there were plenty of boats in the water to be involved, as well.

In fact, festivities seemed to have already begun, as not only were the contestants delivered to the docks by boat, but a man dressed as King Neptune, as well. Neptune arrived on a barge surrounded by twenty women in costume, and twenty black men dressed as Nubian slaves.

Once King Neptune and his subjects were on the docks, the second barge brought the beauty queens in. There were eleven of them, O'Farrell knew, because Georgie Taylor would have been the twelfth. Apparently, her death had gone unreported to pageant officials, who had not had time to replace her, or they'd been surprised when she hadn't arrived and had gone ahead with eleven.

The contestants were allowed to wear their new risqué bathing suits on the barge, showing lots of skin, but were then whisked away to don something more appropriate for the party.

"Well," Bat said, when the girls were gone, "it won't be easy judging the most beautiful out of that lot, tomorrow night. I'd better find the officials and ask them what they want me to do."

"I'll see you inside the tent, then," Val O'Farrell said.

"Better stick with me, Val," Bat said, "at least until I get you introduced to someone in the know."

That was wise, O'Farrell knew. On his own he might end up being kicked out before he could find Vincent Balducci.

"Good idea."

8

The pageant officials pinned a button on Bat's lapel identifying him as a judge, and agreed to give O'Farrell some sort of a guest button. So armed, both O'Farrell and Bat joined the party in the tent.

There was a stage with a big band on it, playing their hearts out while a male and female singer alternated songs.

Guests in various stages of dress were filling a dance floor, or milling about holding champagne glasses or martinis or wine, all of which was being circulated by uniformed waiters. Money had been paid out, whether it was for a license, or just a bribe, but the giggle juice was flowing freely.

The men were wearing expensive suits and, in some cases, tuxedoes. The women flaunted jewelry—rings, bracelets, even tiaras—and the fashions of the day, in some cases their six-inch hems flying even higher while they danced the Charleston, the Shimmy, the Fox Trot or even the Black Bottom. It seemed as if many of the women who were young enough to care thought they had to do something to compete with the bathing beauties. Indeed, O'Farrell realized some of the women on the dance floor were the contestants, themselves. He could imagine Georgie out there dancing among them, and it made him angry—angrier than he'd been since he first discovered her body.

A male singer started to sing "My Time is Your Time," and couples moved in closer to dance together.

"See him?" Bat asked.

"Who?"

"Your client?"

"Not yet."

"I see somebody you know," Bat said, pointing to Detective Sam McKeever of the New York Police Department, who was fast approaching with another man in a suit and some uniformed New Jersey police in tow. Right on time.

"Val," McKeever said, "this is Detective Willoughby of the Atlantic City Police."

"What did you find out?" O'Farrell asked McKeever, after tossing Willoughby a nod.

"She was killed sometime Thursday night. Both doormen have alibis," McKeever said. "They were both seen on duty by other tenants."

"They could have slipped away long enough to kill her," Bat offered.

"You're muddying the waters again, Bat," O'Farrell said. "There are three logical suspects for this crime."

"And you've cleared the doormen?" Bat asked, looking at

McKeever.

"Yeah," McKeever said, then, "Hey, you're Bat Masterson."

"At your service," Bat said.

One of the uniformed police said to the others, "That's Bat Masterson."

O'Farrell saw Bat's chest inflate until another officer said, "Who's he?" and a third said, "Newspaperman, I think."

"Did you manage to keep this from Lieutenant Turico?" O'Farrell asked.

"Yeah, but he ain't gonna like it."

"I wanted you to get the collar," O'Farrell said.

"Wait a minute," Bat said. "You said there were three logical suspects—"

"Well," McKeever said, "four, but I'm clearin' Val, here."

"Okay," Bat said, "so if you've cleared Val, and the two doormen, that leaves—"

"There he is," O'Farrell said cutting Bat off. He started to push through the crowd, causing several people to spill their drinks.

"Follow 'im," McKeever said to the other cops, and Bat followed them.

O'Farrell was faster than they were, though, and was not being careful about who he bumped. As he got closer, Vincent Balducci turned and saw him coming towards him. The millionaire was impeccably turned out in a black tuxedo, and was holding a champagne glass. He was chatting with some people—one of whom was a matronly lady covered in jewels doing nothing to hide the fact that she was *not* one of the contestants. He frowned when he saw O'Farrell coming towards him, then saw something in the detective's face he didn't like. He turned and started pushing through the crowd. O'Farrell increased his speed, leaving McKeever and Bat and the other police to struggle through the crowd behind him.

The band started playing an up tempo number and people started doing the Charleston, again. Balducci was trying run, now, and as he burst out onto the dance floor a heavyset woman trying to keep up with the music slammed into him with her hip and sent him flying across the floor. He bumped into a man whose arms and legs were flailing about in an obscene caricature of the dance and they both fell to the floor. The man shouted, but Balducci—in excellent physical condition—jumped up and began running again. He got a few steps when a slender but energetic girl in a flapper's dress banged into him with a sharp-boned hip and knocked him off balance. He managed to stay on his feet and finally made his way across the dance floor to the exit next to the bandstand.

O'Farrell, following in his wake, managed to avoid all the traffic Balducci had encountered and was right behind him.

It was dark out and Balducci headed for the marina. O'Farrell wasn't even sure why the man was running, but he took his .45 from his shoulder holster just the same.

The millionaire ran to the end of a dock, then turned to face O'Farrell.

"You can't shoot me!" he cried out, waving his hands. "I'm not armed."

"Why would I want to shoot you, Vincent?" O'Farrell asked. He holstered his gun. "In fact, why are you running from me?"

Balducci was sweating so much that some of the dye from his hair was running down his forehead.

"Wh-why were you chasing me?"

"Was I?" O'Farrell asked.

"You came at me...the look on your face...I thought..."

The man was too fit to be winded from running. He was out of breath for another reason.

Suddenly, there was a small automatic in his hand. O'Farrell cursed himself to holstering his gun.

"I—I didn't mean to," Balducci said. "She told me about the sex... and I just went crazy... it wasn't my fault."

"Is that the gun?" Georgie had been shot at close range with a small caliber gun. "Where'd you get it?"

"It was hers," he said. "I gave it to her for protection. I—I never thought she'd try to use it against me."

"You must have frightened her."

"She... she was mine! She wasn't supposed to be with anyone else."

O'Farrell felt badly about that. Maybe if he hadn't slept

with Georgie she'd still be alive now, or maybe it would have happened later, with someone else.

"Come on, Vincent," O'Farrell said. "If you shot her by accident, then you're not going to shoot me deliberately."

"You know," Balducci said, "you know... I knew it when I saw your face. I—I can't let you tell anyone."

O'Farrell wondered where the damned police were? And where was Bat Masterson? He was wondering how close he'd get to his gun if he tried to draw it now.

"Vincent—"

"I'm sorry," Balducci said, "I had no idea it would come to this when I hired you. I'm so sorry..."

Balducci tensed in anticipation of firing his gun, but before he could there was a shot from behind O'Farrell. A bullet struck Balducci in his right shoulder. He cried out and dropped his gun into the water, then fell to his knees and clutched his arm. O'Farrell turned to see Bat Masterson standing at the end of the dock with an old Colt .45 in his hand. He turned to check that Balducci was neutralized, then walked over to Bat.

"Thanks, Bat."

"I still got it," Bat said.

"Where'd you get that?"

"Hey, all the guns in my desk aren't harmless replicas, you know."

Behind Bat, Sam McKeever came running up with the other policeman.

"Damned Charleston," he said. "How'd you get across that dance floor without slamming into somebody?"

"I'm graceful."

"Did he do it?"

"He did it," O'Farrell said. "He confessed. I'll testify, but I don't think I'll have to."

The other detective, Willoughby, waved at his men and said, "Go get him."

"You'll need divers," O'Farrell told both detectives. "The gun fell in the water when Bat shot him."

"The same gun?" McKeever asked, surprised.

"Yeah," O'Farrell said, "for some reason he was carrying

it around. He said he gave it to her for protection."

The uniformed police helped Balducci to his feet and started walking him off the dock. When they reached O'Farrell and the two detectives, they stopped.

"I'm sorry I slept with her, Balducci," O'Farrell said. "It just happened, but she shouldn't have died for it."

Balducci's mouth flopped open and he said, "You slept with her, too?"

As they marched him away McKeever said, "One of the doormen. Apparently he went up there when Balducci wasn't around."

"So he didn't know about me and her," O'Farrell said.

"He does now," McKeever said.

"And so do we," Bat said.

"You dog," McKeever said.

"I wonder if his money will be able to buy him out of this?" Bat asked.

"Don't matter to me," McKeever said. "My job's just to bring 'im in."

Bat and McKeever started after the other policemen. Let them rib him, O'Farrell thought, bringing up the rear. It wasn't his fault she was dead. That's what counted. Now he could be sad for her, and not feel any guilt.

Tequila Spike
Anonymous-9

I prayed for help, but help never came. By the time you read this, I'll be dead. I'm going to kill her first... and once the kid is safely on the bus... I'm going to finish me. I'm writing this to prove that if you were in my place, and saw what I saw, and knew what I knew, for sure, for sure... you'd kill her, too.

"Thweeeeeet..."

The door sensor goes off as a woman enters the store towing a little kid. It's my first week as a clerk, and I still pay attention to faces. Anyway, she's pretty in a messy kind of way, wearing sweats that've been around too long, and smoking a super-long menthol. Her makeup looks fresh, even though it's pretty thick for ten in the morning. She says "hi" in a raspy voice, not loud. The kid, a girl about five years old, doesn't look at me, and goes straight for the donut case.

"She's going to pick out what she wants to eat," the woman says. "Her name is Chloe."

She sticks out her hand. Like I said, I was still pretty new, so I stretch my hand across the counter and shake. I catch the kid's name but not hers.

They come in every morning for donuts and soda. Chloe's always quiet; no acting up. They never try to steal anything but I figure something's off when the mom starts a story and never finishes before beginning another... like she's topped up with secrets, but holding back. Says she's on disability but not what for. Something about the social worker doesn't know she has Chloe and it's better that way because she doesn't want interference.

If she stays too long talking at me in that crackly, rapid-fire whisper of hers, it makes me dizzy.

I sort of notice she's dragging the kid around at all hours. Says Chloe has insomnia, just like her. I don't know, the kid sure looks sleepy to me. I feel worry take root inside my gut, which bothers me because it's pointless. What can I do?

She starts asking me to baby-sit. Chloe and I go to the park and play sand castles with empty ice-cream containers. We glue popsicle sticks together and make picture frames. I have a room at the back of the store. Everything is calm back there and daytime quiet. Sometimes I leave the back door open so Sacramento sunshine throws a big yellow square on the floor. Chloe lays inside it and puts puzzles together. Finished, she turns her little face up and says, "Did I do good, Bebbie?" My name is Bebbie, like Debbie only with a B.

I tell her, "Yes, Chloe, you did good. You did very, very good." We kick back and float on the day, suspended in time and sunbeams.

Was I lonely before Chloe? I never thought so. But now, when she's not with me, the time just seems so... empty.

"Thweeeeet..."

A boyfriend starts showing up with the mom. A white guy with a black eye, fading. He fondles the mom's ass right in front of everybody. I pretend I'm straightening packs of cigarettes, so my face doesn't show my disgust.

I'm glad men don't notice me. Mousey brown hair, tied back. Bangs always flipping the wrong way, no matter how hard I fight them. My store apron doesn't help my figure much. It bunches up and cuts me in two, like a bed pillow tied in the middle. But I have to wear it and they didn't hire me for looks. I make the cash work out, end of every day.

The next time they come in Chloe has strips of a sheet tied around her feet. I don't hide my face this time.

The mom declares, "She got burnt on the pavement. It was hot."

"How did it happen?"

"We were hitchin' a ride and got into a fight with the

driver, so we had to get out. I didn't know the pavement was hot. And Chloe was in bare feet. Got the hotfoot, didn'cha Clo?"

"Has she seen a doctor?"

"She never needs a doctor. She's a good girl."

I look for the kid's reaction, but her face is set like cement. That kid knows how not to make trouble. She's been trained, for sure.

I find a tube of ointment and hand it to the mom with her donut and soda. "Put this on her feet. It'll help." The mom says thank you and they leave. I feel the worry root grow another inch inside my gut.

A week later the white guy is replaced by a gang banger with tattoos on his neck and hands. Up close at the cash register, his jacket flops open, and I see a holster under his arm. He lets Chloe skip out the door without taking her hand and dammit it if she doesn't scoot right into the parking lot. A van squeals its brakes and stops an inch away from her. The mom and him act soooo surprised and snotty—like cars aren't supposed to be driving in the parking lot. I imagine Chloe lying under the wheels of the van, with dirty bandages on her feet.

The banger stays around for a while, but after a couple months he stops showing up and I stop keeping track. There's a passing parade with the mom—the kind of people circling the drain who haven't made the final flush yet. One time a bleach blonde comes in with them and buys an apple. I'm happy 'cause it's probably the first time Chloe's ever seen a person eat a piece of fruit. Bleach-Blo pulls out a stiletto blade and starts slicing bits of apple and eating them right off the blade. Four or five slices in, the stiletto slips and cuts her deep between the thumb and forefinger. Blood shoots clear across the aisle and sprays a shelf of spaghetti sauce. You should've heard the hooting and howling. Chloe doesn't cry or say anything at all. But her little face is white, shock white.

* * *

I pray at night, even though I don't really believe in it. *Please help me come up with something. Please, please don't let the kid get hurt.* You have to understand; I never had a kid in my life before. I hear prayers get answered sometimes, and I figure it's probably like playing the lottery. If you don't buy a ticket, you can't win. So I pray anyway, for Chloe.

The mom wants an afternoon alone with one of the drain-riders. It's my day off and I agree to come by. They live at the El Morada Motor Hotel, a squat row of units with parking strips painted outside. You can rent by the week. The minute I step inside, my sinuses fill up. The room hasn't been cleaned since Saddam got pulled out of the rabbit hole. Heck, the place *looks* like Saddam's rabbit hole. Junk, garbage and crumbs everywhere. It stinks. The room explains everything. It explains too much.

The mom hands Chloe over to me, babbling how good it is to go out on a date and have some time to herself, blah, blah... We go to feed pigeons. A couple loaves of bread from the store are precious to Chloe. She can sit and feed birds forever. When her stash gets halfway down, she starts tearing pieces smaller so they'll last longer. I love watching her take care of birds.

"Did I do good, Bebbie?"

"Yes, honey, you did real good."

I call Child Protection and here's how it goes down. They respond right away, but because there's no immediate danger, *translation: no blood and bruises*, they can't act. Instead, they tell the mom they'll be back in a week to "check out the environment." That's the law, right to privacy. Guess what happens... can you guess? The day the social worker comes, the mom rents a kitchenette with a bedroom nook, so it looks like Chloe has her own bed. The mini-fridge has bologna and ranch dressing inside, so it looks like there's food. The worker reports it as "a low income but satisfactory environment." And that's that. Next day, Chloe's back in the hellhole.

I try to accept the verdict. I tell myself that I've done the most anyone can do. The law has intervened and the law says it's okay. But that worry plant is so tall inside my guts it's pushing up my throat. When whatever is bound to happen finally happens, I won't be able to live with myself. Did you catch that? *I won't be able to live.*

My next thought is about killing.

I go around and around on how to do it. I'm pretty sure I can get the job done and get away with it, but Chloe is the problem. How do I just show up with a kid? Even if we move away, I'll get asked for a birth certificate and questioned about medical records and all that. Without ID they'll peg me for one of those child molester-kidnappers. I have to let go of wanting Chloe, or anything for myself, and just concentrate on what's best for her. Once I get my head wrapped around that the rest is easy.

I make a few calls and discover that in the state of California orphans hit the jackpot. With no family standing in the way, the good life rolls up on wheels and takes the kid in, day or night. She gets new clothes, food, toys, and a temporary home—somewhere clean, safe, and the caretakers all checked out. The state starts an immediate search for a family to permanently adopt. The good-life-on-wheels has money for everything you can imagine—medical, dental, and special help with school. The way things are going, I don't think Chloe is ever going to *get* to school, so this sounds like a dream come true.

There's just one thing standing in the way of the jackpot and Chloe... and you know who that is by now, don't you?

I decide to poison her.

Low-key, no trauma, no drama... no violence for Chloe to witness. Chloral hydrate. Spiked in a bottle of liquor. I've had it forever and remembered it when that blonde billionaire widow Anna Nicole Smith—may she rest in peace beside her son—made it famous. I'll tell Chloe that Mommy's sleeping— I won't say *forever*—and put her in front of the TV with a donut while I quietly call 911. When emergency crews arrive at a situation, the first thing they do is remove the children. As soon as Chloe goes outside with a rescue worker, there will be a minute while they check the mom for vital signs. In that little space, I'll step into the bathroom and put a bullet in my head. Okay, let me bring you up to speed here 'cause you're surprised. *I have to go down the same time as the mom.* The law will nail me sooner or later, and Chloe needs all the bad stuff in her life to be over in one day... so she can get on the bus to a new life with no loose ends pulling her any way but forward.

I'm not afraid to die. I'm not dying for nothing.

It's evening, and I invited myself over to the El Morada. The mom's latest lowlife took off and she's alone, so now's the time. I already put the Anna Ni-chloral hydrate in a bottle of tequila. I got Mr. Bubble for Chloe and a big new bath towel. The towel is wrapped around a gun—a handgun from the store that the owner leaves behind the counter just in case. I'm going to ask the mom if I can give Chloe a bath before bed, and while I'm in there, hide the gun under the bathroom sink for when I need it in the morning...

"Knock knock."

Chloe knows I'm coming and throws herself into my arms. The mom is right there, all smiley when she sees the tequila. I give it to her and she starts rummaging for a couple plastic cups while Chloe and I go into the bathroom and get the Mr. Bubble going in the rusty old tub.

Chloe gets in and lathers up, playing with the foam, and I know it's the right moment to get that gun shoved way back under the sink. So far so good... and all of a sudden the outside door busts open like somebody put a boot through it and a voice hollers, "*You whore,*" and stuff about *acting like a taconera while I been away,* and there's a little *zhzhzhoot* sound like a shot. Somebody hits the wall right next to the bathroom door and makes a soft sliding sound all the way down.

I meet Chloe's eyes—wide and shiny with fear. My fingers go to my lips, a silent shhhh, and I inch the shower curtain across to hide her. Steps come up to the bathroom door—the impact sprung it open a few inches. I'm glued to the sound of those feet and I'm too freaked to even think about reaching for the gun under the sink. A drip from the tap hits the bathwater. It sounds like a firecracker going off. My eyes focus beyond the crack in the door and I see the mom's torso—and a man's hand reaches out to touch her. I recognize tattoos on that hand. And then his face draws near until his eye appears in the door crack. "Come out," he says. The barrel of a gun rises to point at me, underneath his eye.

My legs won't move—knees rubbery, not responding. "Out," he says, again.

If it wasn't for all the blood, the mom could just be taking a nap, sitting all relaxed like that. Except for the bullet through her heart. She has an empty plastic cup in one hand and my tequila in the other. The banger recognizes me, smirks, and crosses to a cheap boom box. A gangsta starts growling about guns and hos—murder music. Banger takes the bottle out of corpse-mom's hand and drinks from it long and hard. "Where's the kid?" he says.

I stutter something about gone with a babysitter while he swigs away. "Tastes like shit," he says, holding the bottle up. It explodes in a thousand sparkling shards. Behind the dazzling spray of tequila, a rose opens in his throat, scattering bloody petals. He staggers back leaving a red swerve on the grimy shag, hits the screen door, and crashes through. Shouts and commotion outside as I look behind me and there is Chloe, little Chloe, naked and dripping, holding a smoking gun. Her small voice sounds innocent and clear, like bird song after a bomb blast, "Did I do good, Bebbie? Did I do good?"

The Rendezvous
A.C. Frieden

September, Northern Ukraine

Tall, dark silhouettes of pine trees, resembling a horde of witches, passed by on both sides of the desolate roadway as the rain pounded Misha's helmet, his soaked gloved hands tightly gripping the handlebars of his old Voskhod motorbike. This was no ordinary night, nor a leisurely ride. The cryptic message spun wildly in his head as he sped along the shoddy pavement, at times weaving into the opposite lane to avoid potholes. *This isn't right,* he told himself, hoping, however, that he'd be proven wrong. That his fear was indeed misplaced. But how could it be?

The text message had in fact come with the proper codewords, and from the right phone number. But everything else in the meeting request was a break from protocol: a rural location not previously used, an ungodly hour that drew unwanted attention when Misha exited the Chernobyl Exclusion Zone checkpoints, and a strange demand to leave his cell phone behind. He'd asked why. He asked for another day and time. But the messenger insisted. Misha had never been tempted to say no before, but even though he needed the money, he'd felt his stomach wrench as he agreed to this meeting. *I can still turn back*, he thought. *I can.*

He reached the town of Ivankiv—an already sleepy hamlet by day, but now, nearing 1:00 A.M., activity was all but nonexistent. He hadn't expected rain, and certainly not this fierce downpour that had soaked through his leather jacket and jeans. The cold wetness of his clothes angered him. If only he hadn't been so rushed. At the village's only lighted intersection, he turned right, heading northwest toward the next village, Obukhovychi.

Misha despised anything rural. The manure-scented air. The primitive dwellings. The peasantry. It reminded him how far his country lagged behind the likes of Austria or Germany, where he'd visited often in recent years. He was in this northern part of Ukraine only by professional obligation, crisscrossing this unimposing landscape after being assigned as the numbers-cruncher at the former Chernobyl nuclear power complex. To him, all that mattered in Ukraine was his native Kiev, and Odessa for those infrequent vacations on the coast, but nothing else. Accountants don't belong in fields or forests, he thought, and even less so on such a dreary night.

The rain pummeled his helmet, muffling the sounds of his bike as he continued down the darkened road walled-in by tall trees—witches, he thought, as his mind raced along with his motorbike. Perhaps they had cast an eerie spell on him. His prior rendezvous had always seemed mundane, and most importantly, safe. But not this one tonight.

"What the fuck am I doing here?" he mumbled into his helmet. He struggled to gauge why a meeting originally set for Saturday in a quiet café on the west side of the capital was now hurriedly pushed forward. Worse yet, in the middle of the night on a barren green spot on a map. He couldn't think of any justifiable reason.

Misha continued down the country road, his weariness exacerbated by nerves. Could it be a trap? Had the message really come from his handler? But the codewords were correct, he reminded himself. He'd deciphered them using the identical formula they'd been working with for months.

In keeping with the instructions, he turned onto the first dirt road after spotting the faded welcome sign for Obukhovychi. His heart sped up the moment he saw the path exit the roadway and enter a forest that looked like a witches' lair. He thought of his handler, a man he knew only as Brian—a wiry, sharp-dressed Brit whom Misha had never imagined would be the type to meet anywhere as uncivilized as a forest.

He slowed. The rain eased the instant he passed under the shelter of the pine trees. He slowed further, maneuvering his bike over the muddy trail and natural debris that told him no one had wandered down this way in a while. It reminded him of his childhood fear of forests—and not just because they were dark and secluded. His grandfather had gone missing on a long walk through the woods and was later found dead of a heart attack. Misha had gone through his teens believing all woods were haunted. As an adult he simply disliked them.

Misha struggled to keep the bike's tires from sinking into the muddy trail layered with fallen branches, wet leaves and shrubs. His boots felt heavy. He peered into the darkness but saw nothing. Then a brief flash of headlights suddenly pierced through the mass of tree trunks ahead. The car must have driven in from another path, since he hadn't seen tire marks.

He stopped about fifty yards from the car but stayed seated on his bike, the engine idling. He noticed his breaths increasing. This spot could not be farther from help, if he needed it. His eyes chased the darkness for any sign of Brian. He removed his helmet, tensely scanning what little he could see.

Misha quickly pondered how he'd escape if things went wrong. *Impossible.* There was no telling who else was around, perhaps behind him, or to the sides, hidden, maybe with a night-vision scope aimed at his head.

An outline of a long-coated person emerged a few feet away and slowly approached.

Misha keenly eyed the silhouette with the scrutiny he would give a financial statement. The person didn't appear to have Brian's lean physique. The man was shorter. Wide-framed.

"Glad you made it, Michael," the man then said in English, barely loud enough to be heard over the 175 cc of motor belching between Misha's legs.

He felt a chill crawl down his spine. That was not Brian, for sure. The Brit had switched to calling Misha by his nickname some months ago.

"Where's Brian?" Misha blurted loudly, his heart now threatening to crush through his sternum. He turned the handlebars toward the stranger and flipped on the high beam. "Where is he?"

"Don't worry." The man instantly covered his face with

his arm, with only his whitish-gray hair showing, and stopped. "Turn off the light!"

"Who are you?" Misha gripped the throttle tightly, revving it twice as he considered making a run for it.

"Turn it off!" He used his other hand to further shield his face. "Brian sent me instead on short notice." His accent was British, but not completely. Misha sensed a trace of Russian or Ukrainian that was not entirely camouflaged.

Misha switched to his native Ukrainian. "I have instructions to only meet with Brian," he said. And it was true. Brian had always said no one else would meet Misha on his behalf.

"I only speak English," the man said, his voice hardening. He casually crossed the beam of the motorbike's headlight, still covering his face. "And please turn off that light. If you don't turn it off, I'll break it."

Misha switched off the headlight as he cast about for an escape plan. "I don't like sudden changes."

"We have our reasons." The man turned briefly to light a cigarette.

"What's your name? Who do you work for?"

"It doesn't matter."

"I will not meet like this again." Misha stared at the stranger's face faintly illuminated by the glowing end of his cigarette the moment he took a long drag.

"It would be easier to talk if you turn off your engine."

"No."

"There is no reason to worry." The stranger took a step closer and another drag of his tobacco. "Do you have the materials?"

"Yes." But Misha suddenly realized that if this meeting were a trap, he'd have no leverage after handing over the thumb drive. "I mean, only some of it. The rest is in a safe place—I'll give it later." He hoped the man would buy the lie.

The stranger stretched out his left hand. "Give it to me."

The hair on the back of Misha's neck stood on end but he struggled to keep his voice steady. "I don't understand what's so urgent. It's only transactions—boring financial records that only people like me appreciate. If Brian can wait a few more days, I'll have better information than I do tonight."

The man expelled a deep smoke-filled laugh and threw down his cigarette.

Misha breathed in deeply and quickly reminded himself of the money. Brian had been generous. He wasn't about to give that up. He dug into his jacket pocket and retrieved the thumb drive. "They are mostly PDFs and a few spreadsheet files." He dropped it into the man's open palm.

"How much more is missing?"

"This is most of the data I told Brian about. As I said, I'll need more time to collect the rest."

The man said nothing. He simply gazed at the USB stick and then closed his fist.

"And my money?"

The man stayed silent.

Despite the cold, Misha felt his armpits grow clammy with sweat. "Brian assured me he'd transfer it to my account in Vienna." Misha thought of his mother's surgery, which he'd paid for last time he'd given Brian names and addresses of key engineers at the Chernobyl complex. "You better clear it up with Brian tonight, because I won't accept silence on this issue."

"How much was your arrangement?"

"Five!" Misha said, insulted he'd have to remind this man of the deal. "Five fucking thousand, you hear me?"

"Euros?"

"No, beers." Misha's anger boiled. "Yes, Euros, what do you think?"

The stranger let out what seemed like a chuckle and then crossed his arms, slowly taking two steps back, the sound of crunching branches breaking the dead air. "Not my problem." He then lit another cigarette. "But I will relay the message." His tone reeked of insincerity.

The cold fear Misha had sensed the moment he'd come into the forest swept back into his head, tempering his rage. He didn't say anything else, his indignation bottled up by self-preservation. But as he watched the stranger pocket the thumb drive, Misha felt a sense of shame wash over himself as well. He had been accustomed to longer, pleasant chats with

Brian, along with the very finest of British civility. A glass of wine, a fine cigar, and even once a game of chess. They'd built a rapport that had comfortably cleansed the soiled reality of an agent-handler relationship. This stranger had exposed the treasonous role Misha had been seduced into playing—a pawn, a mere microscopic cog in a slimy wheel of a major power's espionage machine. And as the stranger turned away, Misha understood that he had very possibly sold out his honor for nothing.

The stranger disappeared into the darkness toward where the car had flashed its lights.

"You're welcome, asshole," Misha mumbled alone as his hands trembled. Before putting on his helmet, he scanned the trees before turning on his bike's headlight, looking for a sniper. The pine needles rustled as he revved the engine and headed out of the forest, sweating through the chill of his still-wet clothes.

A long stretch of desolate, rain-soaked roadway in the near pitch-black night is a lonely, scary place when you're on the payroll of a foreign power, betraying your employer—and your country—by turning over official financial records. This sullied truth clung to him like the mud on his motorcycle boots. Misha's heart was still racing as he watched the speedometer needle vibrate over the one hundred kilometers per hour mark—about as fast as he could go on this battered rural road. The rendezvous bothered him. Had he just been duped? He replayed the stranger's voice in his head. Brian had always reminded Misha of the sensitive nature of his role, something that had to be kept secret from his Ministry—and from anyone else, for that matter.

But if he'd been duped, he'd be dead by now, he surmised. Misha forced his thoughts to slow down. As the distance away from the witches' lair increased, his heartbeat seemed to steady itself. The stranger had broken protocol, but he hadn't harmed or threatened Misha. Indeed, Brian must have sent him. He was now sure of it, and once he was home, he'd message Brian to make sure everything was proper.

The rain beat down as Misha sped up to reach his destination. All he wanted now was to be back in his apartment, in the relative safety of the Exclusion Zone. As he sped along the road, his body shook, the cold heaviness of his soaked clothes nearly unbearable. He squinted, quickly wiping his visor with his gloved hand. There was something ahead. He wiped again with his sleeve.

A wire!

He instantly squeezed the brakes but knew even as he did so that he couldn't stop in time. He slammed into the wire stretched chest-high across the road.

Thump!

He flipped backwards, catching a glimpse of his legs flinging upward as he twisted airborne, the bike darting forward from under him. His helmet smashed onto the pavement, the rest of his body following, the impact on his ribs knocking the wind out of him. He rolled four or five or six times before coming to rest in a motionless state.

Misha heard his own rapid panting echo in his helmet, his breaths steaming the cracked visor. The pain hadn't arrived yet, which surprised him. His lungs pumped out short wheezes. The raindrops hammered his helmet. The motorbike's engine whined in the background. But no pain.

No pain because suddenly he realized he couldn't feel a thing below his shoulders. His legs were numb. His arms and hands, too. No pain, no tingling, no cold, no wetness. Nothing. He tried to yell but couldn't push more than faint puffs of air out of his mouth.

He clenched his jaw and turned his head, barely. His body lay face down on the pavement. All he could see was the soaked asphalt through his cloudy, shattered visor.

Suddenly, the sound of another engine approached from somewhere behind him, and the wet asphalt glowed from a beam of light. A car, he guessed. He heard two doors open and close. The engine idled. His Voskhod suddenly went silent. Muffled voices echoed amid the sounds of rapid footsteps sloshing over the wet road. Misha tried desperately to move, but every appendage remained numb. He wheezed out a weak cry and juggled his head back and forth, attempting to bring the vehicle into his line of sight, but to no avail. The drenched pavement was all he could fixate on as he heard what sounded like two or three people pacing near him. But none came to his aid.

"Break his neck," he heard a man shout.

"No!" Misha coughed out his lungs, realizing they were not rescuing him. They were going to finish him off.

A shadow loomed into Misha's narrow line of vision.

He screamed. "*Nyet!*"

Excerpt from the forthcoming thriller, THE PYONGYANG OPTION, which is the third espionage novel in Frieden's Jonathan Brooks series.

ABOUT THE CONTRIBUTORS

Anonymous-9

Down & Out Books released *Bite Harder* in trade paperback, on October 15th, 2014. The sequel to *Hard Bite*—about a paraplegic vigilante who tracks hit and run drivers in Los Angeles with the aid of a deadly service monkey— won a Readers' Choice Award 2012 from the House of Crime and Mystery (Canada) and was listed in the Top 5 Debut Novels of 2013 by Mysterypeople/Bookpeople (USA). Short stories by Anonymous-9 have earned Spinetingler Magazine's Best Short Story on the Web 2009, a Thriller Award nomination by a judging panel of the International Thriller Writers, and two Derringer nominations. The author writes in Los Angeles, parties in Texas, and traces her DNA back to Vikings in Scotland. Anonymous-9 is the pen-name of Elaine Ash. Find out more at www.anonymous-9.com.

Trey R. Barker

Trey R. Barker's fiction has been called "... a bloody Revelation— Old Testament style, Baby," by Jay Bonansinga. Ken Bruen said Barker was "... one of the truly original new writers... with style, humor, originality... and a dark wicked sense of pace and plotting."

His Barefield novels—published by Down & Out Books—blast through the American southwest at a bit more than a hundred miles an hour. *2,000 Miles to Open Road, Exit Blood*, and the forthcoming *Death Is Not Forever* are exercises in families gone awry, with blood and bullets and backstabbing galore.

Slow Bleed, his recent novel, gives his fans a surprisingly different voice from this master of stripped down, hardboiled prose. *Slow Bleed* is more thoughtful, though it doesn't slow down and doesn't spare Barker's continual exploration of people on the edge of the abyss.

Barker lives in north-central Illinois and is a sergeant with the Bureau County Sheriff's Office and is a member both the Illinois Attorney General's Internet Crimes Against Children Task Force and the Quad Cities Cyber Crimes Federal Working Group.

Rob Brunet

Rob Brunet's 2014 debut, *Stinking Rich*, asks *What could possibly go wrong when bikers hire a high school dropout to tend a barn full of high-grade marijuana?* His award-winning short crime fiction appears and is forthcoming in Thuglit, Ellery Queen Mystery Magazine, Shotgun Honey, Out of the Gutter, Noir Nation, and numerous anthologies. Before writing noir, Brunet produced award-winning Web presence for film and TV, including *LOST, Frank Miller's Sin City*, and the cult series *Alias*. He loves the bush, beaches, and bonfires and lives in Toronto with his wife, daughter, and son.

Tom Crowley

Tom Crowley is the author of *Bangkok Pool Blues*, a non-fiction look at the counter culture of the pool world in Bangkok and the denizens who inhabit it. His second book moved into the realm of fiction with his Matt Chance thriller series. The action/adventure work *Viper's Tail* was released by Down & Out Books in September of 2013. A follow up, *Murder in the Slaughterhouse*, was released in August 2014.

Frank De Blase

Frank De Blase is an award-winning writer, photographer, ex-rockabilly crooner, social contrarian, and all-around troublemaker who always leaves room for dessert. His writing and photography has been published in *Leg Show, Leg World, Swank, Ultra, Temptress, Retro Lovely Taboo, Ol' Skool Rodz, Car Kulture Deluxe, Rebel Ink, Skin and Ink, Urban Ink, V Magazine*, and *Downbeat*. De Blase is a monthly contributor to *Crimespree Magazine* as well.

In his tenure as senior music writer at *City Newspaper*, he has been a three-time AAN, Association of Alternative Weeklies, award winner for excellence in music journalism.

De Blase's first novel *Pine Box for a Pin-Up* and his short story collection *Busted Valentines and Other Dark Delights* were published by Down & Out Books. His second novel *A Cougar's Kiss* is forthcoming from Down & Out Books.

With an affinity for the pulp/noir writing style, De Blase's style strolls down the dark side of the street. He has sat on author panels at NoirCon in Philadelphia and Bouchercon in Albany. He has been invited back to both for 2014 and will also be teaching a crime fiction writers course at Writers and Books in New York this fall with his friend and fellow writer, Charles Benoit.

De Blase lives in Rochester, New York with his wife, Deborah.

Les Edgerton

Les Edgerton has a bit of an unconventional background in that he's an ex-con, having spent a bit over two years in prison for burglary, armed robbery, strong-armed robbery and possession with intent to sell. He also was a pimp, acted in porno movies, sold and used drugs, was in several shoot-outs and chases with cops, worked for an escort service, was the subject of several attempted stabbings and shootings by his girlfriend a call girl, was friends with the nephew of the New Orleans Godfather, Carlos Marcello, and had lots of fun adventures. Then, he went to college, got his B.A. from I.U., and an MFA in Writing from Vermont College and married his fifth wife who was "the one" and settled his ass down. His 18th book has just come out from Down & Out Books, a black comedy crime caper titled *The Genuine, Imitation, Plastic Kidnapping* and he's doing a final edit to a memoir, *Adrenaline Junkie*, which the president of HBO Films called "... a *Permanent Midnight* but with balls."

A.C. Frieden

A.C. Frieden is an international author of globetrotting legal and spy thrillers, including the acclaimed Jonathan Brooks series. Frieden is also an intellectual property attorney, private pilot, divemaster, martial artist, equestrian, former biologist and army sniper. He was born in Africa and lived in India, Switzerland and the UK before moving to the U.S. and has visited over 70 countries, including North Korea, Cuba, Russia, Venezuela, Ukraine and other hotspots, many of which are settings in his novels. His next thriller, *The Pyongyang Option*, is set in Chernobyl, Ukraine and in the North Korean capital, two places Frieden has extensively researched during his travels. He speaks French, English, Portuguese, Spanish and some Russian, and carries several passports. He is a member of

Mystery Writers of America, the International Association of Crime Writers, and the Military Writers Society of America. www.acfrieden.com

Jack Getze

Former Los Angeles Times reporter Jack Getze is Fiction Editor for Anthony nominated Spinetingler Magazine, one of the internet's oldest websites for noir, crime, and horror short stories. His Austin Carr Mysteries *Big Numbers* and *Big Money* were reissued by Down & Out Books in 2013, with the new *Big Mojo* set for 2014. His short stories have appeared in A Twist of Noir, Beat to a Pulp and The Big Adios.

David Housewright

A reformed newspaper reporter and ad man, David Housewright has published 16 crime novels including *The Devil May Care*. His book *Penance* earned the 1996 Edgar Award for Best First Novel from the Mystery Writers of America as well as a Shamus nomination from the Private Eye Writers of America. *Practice to Deceive* (1998), *Jelly's Gold* (2010), and *Curse of the Jade Lily* (2013) have each won Minnesota Book Awards. Housewright has also published a collecting of short stories entitled *Full House* (Down & Out Books). He was elected President of the Private Eye Writers of America in 2014. In addition, Housewright has taught novel-writing courses at the University of Minnesota and Loft Literary Center in Minneapolis, MN.
Website: www.davidhousewright.com.

Bill Moody

Jazz drummer and author Bill Moody has toured and recorded with Maynard Ferguson, Jon Hendricks, and Lou Rawls. He lives in northern California where he hosts a weekly jazz radio show, and continues to perform around the Bay Area. He is the author of seven novels featuring jazz pianist-amateur sleuth Evan Horne and two spy novels. Additionally, Bill has also published a dozen short stories in various collections. http://www.billmoodyjazz.com/

Gary Phillips

Raised deep amid the cracked concrete and weathered palms of South Central L.A., weaned on the images of Kirby and Steranko in comic books, and Hammett and Himes in prose, Gary Phillips also draws on his experiences ranging from community organizer, teaching incarcerated youth, to delivering dog cages in writing his tales of chicanery and malfeasance. For Down & Out Books, he edited the original anthology *Scoundrels: Tales of Geed, Murder and Financial Crimes* and *Treacherous: Grifters, Ruffians and Killers*, a collection of his crime and mystery stories.

Robert J. Randisi

Robert J. Randisi is the author of the "Miles Jacoby," "Nick Delvecchio," "Gil & Claire Hunt," "Dennis McQueen," "Joe Keough," and "The Rat Pack," mystery series. *The Honky Tonk Big Hoss Boogie*, the first book in the Auggie Velez Nashville P.I. series, appeared in 2013. *Upon My Soul* (2013) is the first book in the "Hitman with a Soul" Trilogy. He is the editor of over 30 anthologies. All told he is the author of over 600 novels, 400 of which are western novels.

He has collaborated with Vince Van Patten (of the World poker Tour) and Eileen Davidson (soap actress on *The Young and The Restless*) on celebrity mystery series.

He is the creator and author of the long running western series *The Gunsmith* as "J.R. Roberts."

He has worked in the Western, Mystery, Sci-Fi, Horror and Spy genres. He is the founder of the Private Eye Writers of America, the creator of the Shamus Award, the co-founder of *Mystery Scene Magazine*, the American Crime Writers League, and Western Fictioneers.

OTHER TITLES FROM DOWN AND OUT BOOKS

See www.DownAndOutBooks.com for complete list

By Anonymous-9
Bite Hard

By J.L. Abramo
Catching Water in a Net
Clutching at Straws
Counting to Infinity
Gravesend
Chasing Charlie Chan
Circling the Runway (*)

By Trey R. Barker
2,000 Miles to Open Road
Road Gig: A Novella
Exit Blood
Death is Not Forever (*)

By Richard Barre
The Innocents
Bearing Secrets
Christmas Stories
The Ghosts of Morning
Blackheart Highway
Burning Moon
Echo Bay
Lost

By Eric Beetner and
JB Kohl
Over Their Heads (*)

By Eric Beetner and
Frank Scalise
The Backlist (*)

By Rob Brunet
Stinking Rich

By Milton T. Burton
Texas Noir

By Dana Cameron (editor)
*Murder at the Beach: Bouchercon
Anthology 2014*

By Tom Crowley
Vipers Tail
Murder in the Slaughterhouse

By Frank De Blase
Pine Box for a Pin-Up
*Busted Valentines and Other Dark
Delights*
A Cougar's Kiss (*)

By Les Edgerton
*The Genuine, Imitation,
Plastic Kidnapping*

By A.C. Frieden
Tranquility Denied
The Serpent's Game
The Pyongyang Option (*)

By Jack Getze
Big Numbers
Big Money
Big Mojo

By Keith Gilman
Bad Habits

(*)—Coming Soon

OTHER TITLES FROM DOWN AND OUT BOOKS

See www.DownAndOutBooks.com for complete list

By William Hastings (editor)
*Stray Dogs: Writing from
the Other America*

By Matt Hilton
No Going Back (*)
Rules of Honor (*)
The Lawless Kind (*)

By Terry Holland
An Ice Cold Paradise
Chicago Shiver

By Darrel James,
Linda O. Johnston
& Tammy Kaehler (editors)
Last Exit to Murder

By David Housewright
& Renée Valois
The Devil and the Diva

By David Housewright
Finders Keepers
Full House

By Jon Jordan
Interrogations

By Jon & Ruth Jordan (editors)
Murder and Mayhem in Muskego

By Bill Moody
Czechmate
The Man in Red Square
Solo Hand
The Death of a Tenor Man
The Sound of the Trumpet
Bird Lives!

By Gary Phillips
The Perpetrators
Scoundrels (Editor)
Treacherous

By Gary Phillips, Tony Chavira
& Manoel Maglhaes
Beat L.A. (Graphic Novel)

By Robert J. Randisi
Upon My Soul
Souls of the Dead (*)
Envy the Dead (*)

By Lono Waiwaiole
Wiley's Lament
Wiley's Shuffle
Wiley's Refrain
Dark Paradise

By Vincent Zandri
Moonlight Weeps

(*)—Coming Soon